ONE NIGHT OF
Scandal

an After Hours novel

ONE NIGHT OF Scandal

an After Hours novel

Elle Kennedy

This book is a work of fiction. Names, characters, places, and incidents are the product of the author's imagination or are used fictitiously. Any resemblance to actual events, locales, or persons, living or dead, is coincidental.

Copyright © 2014 by Elle Kennedy. All rights reserved, including the right to reproduce, distribute, or transmit in any form or by any means. For information regarding subsidiary rights, please contact the Publisher.

Entangled Publishing, LLC
2614 South Timberline Road
Suite 105, PMB 159
Fort Collins, CO 80525
rights@entangledpublishing.com

Edited by Gwen Hayes
Cover design by Bree Archer
Cover photography by Artem Furman/Shutterstock

Manufactured in the United States of America

First Edition September 2014

ENTANGLED
BRAZEN

To Gwen, for your support, your enthusiasm, and most of all, your friendship.

Chapter One

Reed Miller hated nightclubs. Which was damn ironic considering he co-owned one of the hottest clubs in Boston, but hey, that was just smart business. When it came to his personal life, a club was the last place he'd ever associate with a good time.

Most of the women he met at nightclubs were already there looking to get laid, and they were more than willing to go back to his place without much effort on his part. For a man who lived for the excitement of the chase, where was the fun in that?

Right now, however, he was chasing an entirely different type of conquest.

Drugs.

Not for recreational use, of course. He wasn't about to poison his body with that crap. Even during his glory days as a mixed martial arts fighter, he'd never once used performance enhancers. Those were a surefire way to not only get kicked off the circuit, but a pathetic attempt to cheat yourself to victory.

Tonight was for reconnaissance purposes only. For the past couple of months, some a-hole had been selling Ecstasy over at Sin, the club Reed operated with his two best friends. None of the customers they'd questioned knew the identity of the pusher, and if they did know, they sure as hell weren't eager to reveal it. But the flow of E needed to be cut off ASAP, before the Boston PD decided to launch its own investigation, which could lead to Sin being shut down indefinitely.

Reed had decided to pay a visit to a rival nightclub in the hope that the patrons there might know something, but the only info he'd succeeded in gathering at the Krib so far was the phone numbers of half a dozen girls he wasn't the least bit interested in.

"Wanna dance?"

A cute brunette in a skintight pink minidress voiced the eager request, sidling up to his table with a daiquiri in her manicured hand. He was about to turn her down, but she looked so damn hopeful he didn't have the heart to disappoint her.

"Sure," Reed relented.

He waited as she set her glass on the table, then took her hand and led her to the crowded dance floor. On a raised platform high above the main room, the DJ was spinning a deafening drum-and-bass track that was more suited for fast, frenetic dancing, but the brunette wasn't interested in *fast*. Instead, she twined her arms around Reed's neck and started grinding into him in a slow, sensual rhythm.

Normally he'd be all over that. A pretty girl rubbing up on his groin? Hell yeah.

Tonight it felt like a chore.

Christ, he was sick to death of random hookups with women whose names he couldn't even remember the morning after. Maybe the fact that he'd just turned thirty was souring him on the whole casual sex scene, or maybe it was seeing his best friends happily involved in committed relationships. With Gage and AJ no longer serving as his wingmen, Reed was all alone in the land of the single, and he was really starting to hate it.

"You're so sexy." His dance partner brought her red-painted lips to his ear and shouted to be heard over the pounding music.

Reed lightly grazed her hips with his hands, trying to ease back from the undulating pelvis that was targeting his crotch like a heat-seeking missile.

"Thanks," he answered awkwardly.

"Wanna get out of here?" A bright flash of strobe revealed the meaningful smile on her face.

"Naah, I'm not ready to leave yet." He raised his voice. "I'm looking for some party favors. Don't wanna go home until I find some."

Interest flickered in her eyes. "Like what?"

"Ecstasy. Do you know if anyone's holding?"

His dance partner's response was swift and unexpected. Previously eager arms dropped from his shoulders, annoyance streaking through her expression as she took an angry step back.

"Seriously? You're into that crap? Ugh! Why does every guy I meet end up being a total tweaker!"

With a loud, unladylike expletive, she huffed off and abandoned him on the dance floor.

How ironically delightful. Rejected by a chick he hadn't even been into.

Torn between groaning in frustration and chuckling with amusement, Reed once again threaded through the mob of sweaty people. He'd intended on returning to his table, but he stopped in his tracks when he spotted a familiar face in the crowd.

Son of a bitch.

Was that *Darcy*?

It was hard to be sure thanks to the wild blinking of the strobe lights and the darkness obscuring her face every other second. Without hesitation, he changed course and headed in her direction. A part of him wished like hell that it was simply a case of mistaken identity.

Because if it *was* Darcy, then he'd just witnessed his best friend's girlfriend *kissing* another man.

No, wait. He squinted, realizing the couple he'd glimpsed wasn't actually kissing. Their faces were close, but they seemed to only be talking.

And yup, it was definitely Darcy Grant. Now that he was five feet away, he was clearly able to make out her features. Wide-set blue eyes, high cheekbones, that sexy mouth—

He forcibly shoved the last thought out of his head. He wasn't allowed to even *think* the word "sexy" in relation to AJ's girl. It was a total violation of bro code.

Then again, who was he kidding? He'd broken the code a hundred times over when it came to Darcy. All those dirty, dirty thoughts he'd had about her pretty much ensured he'd be going straight to shitty friend hell.

At the moment, though, he was more concerned with why AJ's girlfriend was flirting with another man. Maybe it wasn't his place to interfere, but damned if he'd let his best friend get played for a fool.

AJ Walsh was the closest thing Reed had to a brother. The two of them had grown up together in South Boston, attended the same schools, played on the same sports teams. Reed would take a bullet for his buddy, and he knew that if their roles had been reversed, AJ wouldn't hesitate to stick up for him.

Squaring his shoulders, he marched up to the couple's table and donned his best death glare. "Hey, Darcy," he said loudly.

Her head swiveled, eyes widening when she recognized him. "Reed!" Her voice came out shrill, and there was no mistaking the guilty note ringing there.

He shifted his gaze to her companion, a lanky man with pale blond hair and a smug grin. "Can we help you?" the guy demanded.

Reed experienced a case of instant dislike. Scowling deeply, he jabbed a finger in the air and snapped, "Get out of here."

The guy's jaw dropped. "No way, man. The lady and I were in the middle of—"

"Nothing," Reed finished. "You were in the middle of nothing. So get lost."

Darcy's companion turned to her with visible wariness. "Is this your boyfriend or something?"

"Or something," Reed answered for her.

Several more seconds ticked by, until the blond guy finally hopped off his stool and glowered at Darcy. "You should have fucking told me you had a boyfriend instead of wasting my goddamn time."

As he stormed off, Reed usurped the empty seat, rested his elbows on the table, and looked at AJ's girlfriend with cold eyes. "What. The. *Fuck*. Is. This?" He could barely get the question out he was so pissed.

Christ. How was he supposed to tell his best friend about this? AJ would be devastated when he learned what his girlfriend was up to.

"We were just talking," Darcy retorted, sounding as mad as Reed felt.

"Bullshit," he shot back. "Whatever this was, it was leading toward a hookup, and we both know it."

"So what if it was?" Her blue eyes blazed. "Yeah, maybe it's kinda soon, but what I do and who I see is none of your damn business! If I want to have a rebound fling with some guy I met at a club, then I'm damn well allowed to!"

Rebound?

Reed furrowed his brows, wondering if he'd misheard her. No way had she and AJ broken up. From the moment AJ had introduced her to his friends, Reed had known that Darcy was perfect for the guy, which only made this messed-up attraction he felt for her a million times more wrong. Her easygoing, bubbly personality suited AJ's equally laidback demeanor, while her adventurous nature balanced AJ's tendency to constantly play it safe.

The fact that she was sexy as hell was only icing on the cake.

AJ's cake. Reed clung to the reminder, as he'd done often ever since AJ and Darcy had started dating. It didn't matter that each time he saw her he wanted to bury his face in her graceful neck and breathe her in. Or that his fingers tingled with the urge to stroke her thick, strawberry-blond waves. Or that his cock damn near burst out of his pants at the thought of sinking into her hot, tight—

AJ's girl, yelled the reprimanding voice in his head.

Right. Didn't matter how hot the woman got him. She was off-limits.

But God, did she ever look gorgeous when she was pissed off.

"And you know what else?" Darcy went on, her fair cheeks flushed with anger. "You're not exactly one to judge. You're the biggest player on the planet! But I guess it's okay for *you* to pick up strangers at nightclubs, right, Reed? But when I, an unattached adult woman, does it, suddenly it's *sooooo* wrong and—"

"You and AJ broke up?" he interrupted.

She blinked in surprise. "What?"

"Did you guys break up?" he repeated through clenched teeth.

Looking bewildered, she offered a nod. "Yeah. Last night. He didn't tell you?"

Reed had trouble thinking clearly, what with the massive doses of shock and confusion spiraling through his body. He realized he hadn't spoken to AJ at all today. And his friend had the weekend off, which was why Reed had been tending bar at Sin before he'd headed over to the Krib. Normally, he handled the business end of things, working up in his office on the club's top floor while Gage handled security and AJ managed the bartending staff.

AJ had planned to go away with Darcy this weekend, Reed suddenly remembered.

But Darcy was here.

Picking up dudes.

"Did you dump him?" he demanded.

Her expression grew sad. "No. It was mutual."

That summoned a groan of disbelief. "Break-ups are *never* mutual."

"This one was." Her lips tightened. "Not that it's any of your business, but AJ and I broke up with *each other*. We both knew it wasn't working, and we both decided to end it."

"Why wasn't it working?"

She raked an exasperated hand through her wavy hair. "I'm not giving you any details, Reed. It's between me and AJ, okay?"

Okay? There was nothing *okay* about any of this. In fact, he seriously needed to walk away, right frickin' now, before the little burst of joy that Darcy's admission had evoked in him turned into something else.

He wasn't allowed to be happy about the breakup. No siree. He was supposed to be sad and upset on his best friend's behalf, because no matter what Darcy said, their parting couldn't have been mutual. The guy was crazy about her, for chrissake.

So are you.

Reed silenced the inner taunt. Nope, not going there. He couldn't deny that he was attracted to the woman, but desire was a fickle thing. Sooner or later it would fade.

Or at least, that's what he'd been telling himself for the past five months.

So far, the heat he felt in Darcy's presence still hadn't cooled, but he was certain it would happen eventually.

It *had* to.

"Anyway, there you have it," Darcy finished. "I'm single again. Woo-hoo. I'm sure you're thrilled to have me out of your BFF's life. And now, as you so graciously put it before, *get lost.*"

He narrowed his eyes. "Why do you want me to go so badly?"

She blew out an irritated breath. "Because I came here to have fun! There's zero chance of that happening when you're around."

Reed didn't budge from his chair.

"I'm serious, go away," she grumbled. "We're not friends, okay? And no guy is going to ask me to dance when you're sitting here scowling at everyo—"

"You want to dance?" he cut in. "Let's dance."

Her jaw fell open. Then slammed shut. Wariness filled her expression, and she looked at him like he'd offered to murder her and dump her body in the river.

He didn't blame her. Truth was, she hadn't been too far off the mark. They *weren't* friends. Mostly because he'd learned early on that the only way to curb this inappropriate attraction was to keep a very cold, very polite distance around the woman.

He couldn't do that now, though. Because if he walked away, he risked Darcy getting hit on by some horny fucker and possibly going home with him. He couldn't, in good conscience, let that happen. Break-ups weren't set in stone, especially when they were less than twenty-four hours old, and Reed knew AJ would be devastated if he tried to win his girl back only to find out she'd already slept with another dude.

"I'm not dancing with you," Darcy said coolly.

He smirked. "Fine, then we'll just sit here in silence, for all I care."

"You're acting ridiculous."

"And you're acting insensitive. If you cared about AJ at all, you'd respect him enough not to screw someone else before the break-up ink is even dry."

Annoyance marred her face. "If I choose to have a rebound, you can't exactly stop me."

"Oh yes, I can. As of right now? Consider me your shadow. I'm not leaving your side, baby doll. Not until I tuck you safely into a cab and watch you speed away. *Alone*." Setting his jaw, Reed slid off the stool and held out his hand. "So are we dancing or what?"

...

Darcy was dumbfounded.

And frustrated.

And unbelievably peeved.

She'd purposely come to the Krib tonight because she'd known there'd be no possibility of running into AJ, and just her luck, she'd run into his best friend instead. A man who'd made it abundantly clear that he didn't like her.

Well, eff Reed. She didn't particularly like *him* either. AJ always insisted that Reed was an awesome guy, singing his praises whenever Darcy said otherwise, but in all the months she'd known the guy, he'd only ever shown her a cold, grumpy side that left a sour taste in her mouth.

Oh, and he was bossy. Who could forget *that* annoying little trait? Certainly not her, because right now that bossiness was throwing a wrench in her plans.

Some women got dolled up for any old occasion, but Darcy wasn't one of them. Nope, there was a reason she'd donned a short dress and punished her feet with three-inch heels—passion.

Yep, passion. With a capital P and everything. She was twenty-seven years old, and not once had she experienced anything remotely close to the elusive P. Granted, that was probably because she only dated nice, wholesome guys like AJ. She couldn't deny that her as-of-yesterday ex was smoking hot, but passionate? Not so much.

On the bright side, at least she didn't have to worry that she'd broken his heart. Despite what his aggravating best friend thought, their break-up really had been mutual.

After more than five months of dating, the two of them could no longer ignore the depressing truth: they were great friends, but terrible lovers.

Darcy had hoped the initial spark between them would eventually ignite into a fiery affair for the ages, but sadly, it had fizzled out faster than a candle in a hurricane. And now, thanks to Reed Miller, her quest for a wild night of passion was equally unattainable.

She swept her gaze over his face, ticked off by how good-looking he was. Actually, correction: he was *gorgeous*. Like be-still-my-heart-and-rip-my-panties-off gorgeous. He had close-cropped black hair and piercing blue eyes, and his features were more rugged than pretty, starkly masculine and incredibly appealing.

And south of the border? Holy moly. He was shredded like lettuce, hard muscles and long limbs and a tight ass you could bounce quarters off.

"Stall as long as you want. I ain't going anywhere, Darce."

His deep, razor-sharp voice snapped her from her inappropriate ogling. Fortunately, he didn't seem to notice she'd been checking him out. His expression displayed a cloud of displeasure mingled with steely determination, leaving no doubt as to how serious he was about cock-blocking her tonight.

Or was it vagina-blocking for girls? She wasn't sure.

"You're being totally unreasonable," she said, raising her voice over the music. "I'm not seeing AJ anymore, which means it's not considered cheating if I happen to meet someone I like."

"Don't care. Won't be happening on my watch."

God. He wasn't going to back down.

Cut your losses, girl. You're not the one-night-stand type, anyway.

The defeated voice in her head was spot on. Hopping into bed with strangers wasn't something she indulged in very often. Or *ever*.

Darcy stifled a sigh. Maybe this had been a mistake from the start. A stupid, spur-of-the-moment decision brought on by her break-up with AJ, which, in all honesty, had seriously bummed her out. Not because she'd lost the love of her life or anything, but because their relationship had been so lacking it only highlighted everything she'd been missing. Everything she craved.

Fun. Laughter. Excitement.

Passion.

Yep, full circle, right back to passion.

"C'mon, quit being a brat."

She felt herself being tugged, blinking to find Reed's fingers curled over her forearm. His hand was big and warm, and utterly impersonal as he guided her to the dance floor.

Darcy swallowed her anger as they maneuvered through the crowd. Fine, if he wanted to act like a macho jerk and be her *shadow*, then she'd let him. Clearly passion wasn't on the table anymore, but fun and dancing were still up for grabs, and she might as well get *something* out of this botched evening. Though maybe just the dancing part. After all, *fun* and *Reed Miller* didn't exactly go together.

The sultry beat pounding out of the DJ's turntables immediately snaked its way into Darcy's blood, and her body responded of its own volition. AJ had hated to dance. Poor guy had no moves, either, but his best friend didn't seem to share that affliction.

To her surprise, Reed wasted no time yanking her toward him. He rested one hand on her hip and began to dance to the pulsing, decadent rhythm as if he'd done it a hundred times before.

His head dipped to her ear, his warm breath fanning over her neck. "Why is your dress so short?" he rasped.

She stiffened at his disapproving tone, glancing down at the silky green dress that nearly reached her knees. "It's not *that* short. Look around us—half these girls are practically naked."

"Half these girls aren't *you*."

"What the hell is that supposed to mean?" she demanded.

Rather than answer, he brought his other hand into play, running it up and down her back as his hips rotated in a slow, addictive rhythm.

Oh boy. He smelled fantastic. Sandalwood, citrus, and something uniquely male flooded her nostrils, giving her a bit of a head rush. And his chest was rock-hard beneath her palms—she wanted so badly to stroke it that she had to redirect her hands to his shoulders in an attempt to quell the temptation. Except his shoulders were equally enticing, big and broad and rippling with power.

AJ was built the same lean, muscular way—she knew it had everything to do with the fact that both men had once been professional fighters—but even though she'd slept with AJ many, many times, her hands had never itched to explore every hard, sinewy inch of his body the way they itched now.

Reed's palm grazed her hipbone at the same time he thrust a thigh between her legs, turning the dance from vaguely sensual to downright erotic. Heat unfurled in Darcy's belly and tingled in her sex, triggering a jolt of shock.

Holy crap. She was dirty dancing with AJ's best friend.

And it was turning her on.

No, wait, that was nuts. She couldn't *actually* be turned on. The sweltering air and the two shooters she'd drunk must be to blame, because there was no way Reed the Jerk Miller was getting her motor running.

When she felt his gaze on her, she tipped her head and was floored by what she found. Blue eyes burning with…jeez, was that desire?

Anger?

Defeat?

It sure as hell looked like all three, but only the anger part made any sort of sense. Reed always seemed pissed off when she was around, which was actually kind of insulting since she prided herself on being a very likable person.

"How long are we going to keep doing this?" he said in a strangled voice.

She frowned. "Doing what?"

"Dancing." Sounding even more tormented, he eased away so their lower bodies were no longer touching, but kept his hands on her hips.

If she didn't know any better, she'd have thought he'd inched back so she wouldn't feel the evidence of his arousal pressing into her belly.

But of course Reed wasn't sporting a stiffy in her presence. The only response she'd ever evoked in him was visible irritation and mild indifference.

The memory of his past behavior was like a splash of cold water to the face, propelling her to release his shoulders and take a hasty step back.

What the hell were they doing, grinding to the music like two people who were actually into each other? They weren't even *friends*.

"You're the one who forced me on the dance floor," she snapped at him. "And you're the one who decided not to let me have fun tonight, remember? So if you don't want to dance with me, then don't. Frankly, I'm not interested, either."

She tossed her hair over her shoulder and flounced off, but she should've known better than to think he wouldn't follow her. He did, hot on her heels as she pushed her way through the crowd toward the exit.

"Darcy—"

"Go away, Reed. You win, okay? You've officially ruined my night and put me in a shitty mood, so now I'm going home just like you wanted. Congratulations."

Shooting him one last glare, she spun on her heel and marched out the door.

Chapter Two

"Darcy, wait. Seriously. Come on, wait up."

She kept up the brisk pace, ignoring Reed's increasingly annoyed shouts from behind her. Her heels snapped on the pavement in an angry *click-clack* as she barreled down the sidewalk. She'd taken five more steps when a heavy hand clapped on her shoulder.

"Must you always be so damn difficult?" His aggravated rumble heated the back of her neck.

Darcy twirled around to face him. "Dude, just go away."

His lips twitched. "Can I at least apologize first, *dude*?"

"No."

He grasped her arm before she could walk away. "What do you mean, *no*?"

"Should I say it in a different language so you can understand? Fine. *Non. Nein. Niet. Nej. Nai.* Um—"

"*Nai*?"

"That's Japanese," she said haughtily. "Duh." "Do I even want to ask why you can say the word *no* in so many languages?"

She blew a strand of hair out of her eyes. "I'm a teacher, Reed. I *know* things."

His deep chuckle sent an unexpected—and extremely unwelcome—shiver scurrying through her. Before tonight, she'd never felt anything even close to warmth or awareness toward this man, but somehow her system had short-circuited, and now she couldn't stop staring at his mouth. His firm and surprisingly sensual mouth.

And all that dark stubble sweeping across his strong jaw... She wanted to run her fingertips over it and feel those bristles scratching her skin.

No, you don't.

Right. Of course she didn't.

God, what on earth did the Krib's bartenders put in their drinks? Those shooters were obviously messing with her head.

"Look," Reed said, "I really am sorry for acting like such an ass. I had no idea you and AJ broke up. I honestly thought you were messing around on him."

He looked befittingly repentant, and Darcy supposed she understood how it could have looked to an outsider who didn't know that she and AJ were kaput.

"Fine." She sighed dramatically. "I forgive you, Reedford."

He made a rumbling sound. "Why do you always call me that? I'm not an English prince."

Darcy laughed. "It makes you sound like you have manners. I like you better that way." She reached into her purse and rummaged around for her tiny can of mace. "Okay, now that everything is all sunshine and rainbows between us, I can go home and not have to lie awake all night plotting your death."

Reed's eyes narrowed suspiciously. "Did you call a cab already?"

"No need. I only live six blocks from here."

"You're planning on walking? At *this* time of night?"

She snickered. "It's barely ten o'clock. I think I'll be just fine."

"There's no way I'm letting you walk home alone." He set his jaw and spoke in a stern tone. "Come on, let's go."

Although she was tempted to argue, she couldn't deny that she'd feel safer having someone along. This part of Boston was by no means sketchy, but as Darcy constantly harped to her students, better safe than sorry.

As they took off walking, Reed was quick with the sarcasm. "Wow," he cracked. "You're not going to rip my head off for having the audacity to walk you home?"

She shrugged. "Naah. I know when to pick my battles."

Since it was the end of August, the temperature was still hot even at night, and the humid breeze felt nice against Darcy's face. The lampposts lining the sidewalk shone down on them and highlighted Reed's rugged features, yet again drawing her attention to his lips. According to AJ, Reed was a major player, and she suddenly had to wonder how many women had had the pleasure of kissing those lips.

Though was pleasure the right word? She got the feeling that he might not be the greatest of kissers. He came off as so cocky and selfish, she wouldn't have been surprised to learn that those qualities extended to the way he kissed.

"Did AJ ever tell you how the two of us met?"

The question caught her by surprise. "No, he didn't. All he said was that he's known you forever."

"He has." Reed's voice contained a faraway note. "I've known him since the first grade, but we didn't officially become friends until we were about nine years old. This one day after school, I was walking home and bumped into a group of older guys. Ninth graders, I think. Somehow I picked a fight with them—"

"*Somehow.*" Darcy snorted.

He shot her an evil look. "Anyway, they pounded on me

real good in an alley on 4th Street, around the corner from the school. I was doing my damnedest to fight back, but I was just a scrawny kid back then. Next thing I know, this other skinny kid comes barreling into the alley."

"AJ?"

"Yup." Reed chuckled. "That crazy mofo threw himself into the fray without a single thought to his own safety, and in a total fluke shot, he knocked the group's leader unconscious. The other guys scrambled to help their friend, and the two of us ran off and ended up in the little park near my house. We were riding the adrenaline high, spent a good hour recapping the entire fight, and after that day, we were the best of friends."

Darcy laughed as she pictured the two young boys bonding over a street brawl. "Of course you were." She paused. "You know, it's still so weird to me that AJ used to be a professional fighter. I mean, he's so laidback and calm all the time. If I hadn't seen footage of his MMA fights with my own eyes, I wouldn't have believed it."

Reed shoved his hands in the front pockets of his black jeans. "Yeah, most people can't picture it because he's so chill on the surface. Underneath it, though? Trust me when I say he can be pretty damn deadly."

They reached a crosswalk and obediently stopped in deference to the red DON'T-WALK sign flashing at them. Darcy couldn't help but shoot Reed a sidelong look, noting in surprise that this was the most relaxed she'd ever seen him.

"Do you ever miss your fighting days?" she asked curiously.

He took a moment to think it over. "Sometimes. But I definitely don't miss the intense training. Besides, whenever I'm in the mood to beat the crap outta someone, all I have to do is call Gage. He's always up for a fight."

The mention of Reed and AJ's friend caused a sliver of worry to prick Darcy's chest. "He's not still fighting for that thug, is he?"

"Naah," Reed answered, "Gage is free and clear now, and spending every free moment with his girl."

Must be nice.

Darcy couldn't stop the rush of envy that washed over her. She'd seen the way Gage looked at his girlfriend. Pure adoration, unadulterated passion.

God, she desperately wanted someone to look at *her* like that.

"This is me." She came to a stop in front of her low-rise building.

With its ivy–covered brick exterior and endless expanse of gleaming windows, her place was a lot nicer on the outside than it was on the inside. Her apartment was so tiny, she could barely take a step without bumping into a wall or piece of furniture, but it was all she could afford on her meager teacher's salary. Maybe, if she ever got tenure and the raise that came with it, she'd finally be able to upgrade to a nicer place.

When she glanced at Reed, she was startled to find his blue eyes glued to her mouth.

He looked as fascinated by her lips as she was by his.

Darcy's heart skipped a beat. Holy moly. The man was staring at her as if he wanted to…kiss her.

But no. She had to be misreading the moment. Reed Miller, thinking about kissing *her*? That was just nuts.

And even more nuts?

She didn't think she'd push him away if he tried.

Wasn't that all sorts of messed up. Not only was he AJ's best friend, but he also happened to be the furthest thing from her type. Reed Miller was a bad boy to the core—oh, she'd heard plenty of stories about him from AJ. Apparently the guy possessed an anything-goes attitude when it came to sex. He also smoked cigarettes, cursed like a sailor, and drove way too fast in that black Camaro of his.

Sure, he was a business owner, too. And he had his own house, so she imagined he must be somewhat responsible since he was able to pay the bills. But she was leery of men like Reed, with their unpredictable nature and innate arrogance and those seductive grins that made a woman forget all the reasons why she shouldn't get involved with him.

On the other hand, nobody said she had to *date* a bad boy. But hooking up with one would definitely be a surefire way to inject some passion into her life.

Though preferably, she needed a bad boy that *wasn't* AJ's friend.

Reed cleared his throat, jerking her from her thoughts. He shifted awkwardly as he said, "I'll wait out here to make sure you get inside okay."

Darcy blinked. His sudden preoccupation with her safety made absolutely no sense to her, and it was what prompted her to finally address the enormous pink elephant that seemed to stomp through every room they were in.

"Why don't you like me?" she blurted out.

Surprise flooded his expression, accompanied by a crease of visible discomfort that cut into his forehead.

"I..." He cleared his throat again. "Who says I don't like you?"

"Your *behavior* says it," she retorted. "Before tonight, you've barely said a single word to me. You don't look me in the eye, you don't laugh at my jokes—when I know for a fact that I am *hilarious*—and every time I come to the club, you run away faster than my friend Shannon's husband does whenever *American Idol* is on. Ergo, I'm pretty sure you don't like me."

"That's not true. I, ah, I like you just fine."

Gee, how encouraging. She'd never heard a more lackluster response in her life.

"Okay. Whatever," Darcy muttered. "I guess it was too much to hope that you would give me a straight answer. It's good to know you like me 'just fine.'"

Gritting her teeth, she climbed the first step to the stoop, but Reed grabbed hold of her hand and tugged her back. "Darcy…" His voice came out raspy. "Look…I really do like you."

She shifted her head, locking her gaze with his. "You do?"

"Yeah. I think you're pretty damn awesome, actually. But…"

It suddenly became hard to breathe. "But what?"

His hand was warm against her skin, his thumb sweeping a light caress over her wrist. "But I…" Torment creased his face. "I have to act the way I do, okay? It's the only way for me to—" A strangled noise popped out of his mouth. "Forget it."

"Reed—"

"I've gotta go," he interrupted, keeping his gaze downcast. "Make sure to lock your door the second you get upstairs."

Before she could open her mouth to protest, he was gone.

Darcy stared at his retreating back in disbelief, tempted to run after him and demand he finish that cryptic sentence.

It's the only way for me to…

To what, damn it?

She watched as his long strides briskly ate up the sidewalk, and once he'd fully disappeared from view, she just stared at the empty street, unable to control the pounding of her heart.

What had just happened? If Reed were anyone else, she might think he'd almost admitted to having a thing for her, except the man had never shown even a smidgen of interest in her in the past.

The logical part of her insisted that she'd misinterpreted this whole night from start to finish, but Reed's enigmatic behavior lingered in her mind and followed her all the way up to her apartment.

And haunted her for the rest of the night.

• • •

Reed showed up at the club earlier than usual the next evening. Sin opened at seven o'clock, but he was in his office by six, hoping that the mountain of paperwork on his desk would distract him from thoughts of Darcy.

Christ, he'd come so close last night to telling her how he felt about her. Standing outside her building, with those big blue eyes focused earnestly on his face, he'd nearly spilled his guts. Blurted out just how badly he wanted to kiss her. Confessed to all those nights he'd lain awake thinking about her. Admitted that seeing her with AJ triggered a burst of crushing jealousy he'd never experienced before.

But at the last second, he'd swallowed the confession, knowing it was one he could never, ever voice.

A man didn't hit on his friend's girl—or his friend's ex. Period.

And AJ's friendship meant way too much to Reed to risk throwing away.

"Hey, you're here early." Gage Holt appeared in the doorway, his eyes flickering in surprise to find Reed at his desk.

Reed cocked a brow. "So are you."

"Yeah, I called a staff meeting for all the bouncers," Gage answered as he entered the office and headed for the sole armchair across from the desk.

"How's Jeff working out, by the way?" Reed asked, referring to the bouncer he'd sent Gage's way a few months back. Jeff was an old buddy of his from the fighting circuit, tough enough to handle the security duties required of him, but not a loose cannon like some of the other MMA folks Reed had crossed paths with in the past.

Gage lowered into the chair, leaning his head back. "He's doing great, actually. One of the best guys we have." His expression clouded over. "I want Jeff and the other boys to watch everyone on the floor tonight like hawks."

"Are we any closer to finding the asshole who's dealing in the club?"

Gage was usually hard to read, but tonight his expression clearly broadcast his feelings on the matter. Anger and annoyance shone there, his mouth set in a tight line as he shook his head in response.

"Oh, and I ran into Vinnie this morning," Gage said flatly. "He told me that the cops are starting to crack down on the club district. They want to stop the flow of drugs in the city, and they're planning on using a heavier hand with all the club owners."

"Vinnie knows we're not dealers," Reed grumbled. "We grew up with the guy, for fuck's sake." In fact, Vinnie was the reason Sin didn't receive a lot of attention from local law enforcement. He'd vouched for Reed and the guys, assuring his superiors that everything the three men did was aboveboard.

"There's only so much he can do for us." Gage made a frustrated noise. "Shit. We've really gotta find this dealer before Sin gets a reputation for being a place that pushes drugs."

"I'm working the bar tonight, so I'll keep an eye out too." Reed hesitated. "Have you heard from AJ?"

"No, but Skyler got a call from Darcy earlier today. Did you know AJ and Darcy broke up?"

He shifted in his chair. "Yeah. I ran into Darcy last night at the Krib, and she told me all about it. I tried calling AJ twice today, but he's not picking up his phone."

"I don't blame him. Dude's probably heartbroken."

"You think? Darcy told me the breakup was mutual."

Gage rolled his eyes. "Breakups are *never* mutual."

"That's what I said, but she insisted it was." Reed didn't offer any more details, afraid that the conversation would veer into dangerous territory if he did.

The last thing he wanted was for Gage to ask questions about his encounter with Darcy. So far, he'd successfully managed to mask his attraction for the woman, but he wasn't sure he could keep up the I-Hate-Darcy charade at the moment. Not when his almost-confession to her last night had left him feeling so raw and exposed.

So he swiftly changed the subject to one he knew Gage wouldn't be able to resist. "How's Skyler doing?"

As expected, Gage's expression softened at the mention of his girlfriend. "She's great."

Reed had to grin. "Still rocking your world every night?"

"Hey," his friend chided, "show some respect. That's the mother of my future children you're talking about."

Gage's staunch certainty brought an ache of longing to Reed's heart. Jeez, he was turning into such a pathetic sap. It wasn't too long ago that he'd been perfectly content playing the field and racking up notches on his sex belt, reveling in the excitement of the chase and all the fun it resulted in.

But seeing Gage happy with Skyler, and AJ seemingly happy with Darcy, had stirred up the most fucked up need for something more meaningful than casual sex.

Except the only woman he was remotely interested in was the one woman he couldn't have.

And even if Darcy *was* on the table, he knew she wouldn't date him, anyway. Why would she? She thought he was a player, an opinion he'd helped shape by hooking up with a revolving door of women in the five months Darcy had been with AJ. And besides, he'd never even been in a real relationship before—what could a guy like him offer someone like Darcy?

Reed pushed aside the bleak thoughts and raised his

eyebrows at Gage. "You've only been dating Skyler a couple months. Isn't it a little too early to call her your forever love?"

The other man's voice rang with conviction. "Oh, it's forever."

"Someone's mighty confident of that."

"Trust me, when you know, you know."

Damn it. Now he needed to change the subject again. His attempt to get his friend talking about light-hearted dirty stuff had been foiled by Gage tossing back the F-word.

The *other* F-word—forever.

Fortunately, Reed's cell phone rang before his buddy could drop more F-bombs, but the wave of relief that washed over him dried up the second he glimpsed AJ's number on the display.

"AJ," he told Gage, his muscles tightening right back up again.

"You can take it. I need to go round up the guys, anyway," Gage replied. "I'll catch you later."

As his partner wandered out of the room, Reed raised the phone to his ear and greeted his other partner. "Hey, man, what's up?"

"Nothing really," came the gruff reply. "I just wanted to make sure you restocked the bar after yesterday's rush."

Reed searched for any false or unhappy note in AJ's voice, but heard none. "Yes, Mom, I restocked the bar," he grumbled.

"Good. I figured you'd forget."

A frown surfaced. "I'm not sure if I should be insulted by how little faith you have in me."

There was a beat, and then AJ spoke up guiltily. "Sorry, force of habit. I'm so used to staying on top of you that I keep forgetting you've finally got your shit together."

This time, the remark didn't offend him. Truth was, he hadn't been very responsible in the past. He'd spent his younger days drinking too much, blowing off work, and thinking himself a big-time hero because he happened to fight pro. But he'd cleaned up his act three years ago, after he and his friends had pooled their winnings together to buy the club. Reed had quickly discovered that once you had a real stake in something—and a bank loan to pay back—you grew up *real* fast.

Nowadays, he spent most of his nights doing inventory and signing other people's paychecks, and he genuinely appreciated that AJ recognized he was no longer the irresponsible, self-absorbed jerk he'd once been.

"Don't worry, Gage and I are handling things on this end." Reed hesitated. "You still taking the weekend off? Or are you coming in now that you and…" He trailed off, uncertain about how to proceed.

But AJ had always been able to read his mind. "Now that me and Darcy broke up, you mean?" There was a pause, followed by a tired laugh. "Let me guess—she told Skyler, and Skyler didn't waste any time telling you and Gage."

"Actually, ah, Darcy told me herself." Reed battled a rush of discomfort. "I stopped by the Krib last night and ran into her there."

He was greeted by silence.

A very long silence.

"You still there, man?"

"Yeah, I'm here." Another pause. "Was she with another guy?"

His fingers tightened around the phone. Crap. Should he tell AJ the truth? Lying to his friends wasn't something Reed did often—if ever—but AJ had sounded so unhappy just now that he didn't want to make him feel worse.

And *ha*—he'd *known* the break-up wasn't mutual. If it had been, there definitely wouldn't be this much tension rippling over the line.

"Naah," Reed finally said. "She was only there to dance."

The lie burned his throat as it exited his mouth, sparking a pang of guilt.

But...was it *really* a lie? In the end, Darcy hadn't gone home with another man, so why upset AJ when Reed had successfully managed to thwart disaster?

"That girl loves to dance," AJ said ruefully. "I always felt like such a tool when she dragged me to all those dance clubs."

"Are you...how are you handling it?" Reed injected a hefty dose of sympathy into his tone. "You're not crying into your pillow and listening to Celine Dion or anything, right?"

A snort sounded in his ear. "Hardly. I'm doing fine, man. Honest. It wasn't working, and we both knew it."

Reed shifted in his chair, his chest tightening uneasily again. He wasn't sure what to say next. He'd never been great at talking about his feelings, or helping others work through theirs. There weren't many people he felt comfortable confiding in, and when he was the one serving as confidant, he couldn't seem to vocalize all those nice, encouraging words they needed to hear.

"Well..." Reed cleared his throat. "If you ever want to talk about it..."

"Yeah, yeah, I know. I'll go to Gage." AJ snickered. "Not that he's a sparkling conversationalist either, but at least he doesn't run out screaming when people start talking about their mushy feelings."

Reed couldn't help but laugh. "Yeah, I kinda suck at it. But seriously, bro, I mean it. If you need to talk, I'm here."

"Thanks, man."

"Hey, you wanna go out for beers soon? After the weekend rush?"

"Sure. Sounds good."

After they'd hung up, Reed leaned back in his chair, feeling like a load had been lifted off his chest. And now he was even more sure of what he needed to do.

This attraction to Darcy?

It needed to be squashed. ASAP. Sleeping with her wasn't an option. Same went for dating. And since neither of those options was available to him, he was simply torturing himself by continuing to obsess over her. The only available course of action was to forget about her. Pretend she'd never walked into their lives.

Of course, that was easier said than done.

And, as he discovered two hours later, the plan was a thousand times more difficult to execute when the person he'd decided to avoid didn't seem interested in doing the same.

"Reed." The woman he'd just vowed to forget strolled right up to the bar, her expression awkward as she shouted his name over the blaring music.

He froze, his hand poised on the bottle of Jack Daniels he was about to pour. "Hey," he called out. "What are you doing here?"

Darcy moved closer, resting both elbows on the shiny black counter. She wore skinny blue jeans and a yellow tank top that complemented both her reddish-gold hair and her vivid blue eyes, and as usual, his groin stirred at the mere sight of her.

"I wanted to talk to you," she called back. She sounded as unenthused as he felt. "Do you have a minute?"

He glanced at the crowd of people milling at the counter, which he was working alone at the moment because Henry and Sue, two of the other bartenders, weren't scheduled to come in for another hour. Sin wasn't usually so busy this early in the evening, but he welcomed the aberration, since it allowed him to put off what was bound to be an uncomfortable exchange.

He didn't know why Darcy had showed up out of the blue, but the sudden flare of determination in her eyes told him he wouldn't like—or maybe like too much—what she'd come here to say.

"Not right now," he said lightly. "I've gotta serve these folks."

"That's okay. I can wait."

With a brisk nod, Darcy headed to the far end of the counter and plopped down on the last unoccupied stool.

Reed stifled a groan. Shit. Evidently she wasn't going anywhere until she said her piece.

Swallowing hard, he tore his eyes away from her and tried to concentrate on pouring a stream of alcohol into the row of shot glasses lined up on the smooth counter. Then he pasted on a smile and turned to serve the waiting customers.

Feeling Darcy's gaze on him the entire time.

Chapter Three

She shouldn't have come here tonight. Nope, she should have stayed home like the smart, careful woman she was, and spent the evening finalizing her class's reading list for the upcoming school year.

But curiosity, along with her tireless obsession with solving mysteries, just happened to be Darcy's kryptonite.

I have to act the way I do, okay? It's the only way for me to…

The only way to *what,* damn it? Reed's mysterious words had kept her up half the night, even though a part of her wasn't sure she wanted to know the rest of that sentence. She wished she could talk about it with Skyler or one of her other friends, but that would mean admitting that she'd put way too much thought into the idea that Reed Miller might be interested in her.

As she sat on her stool and fiddled with the straw poking out of her Coke, her gaze kept wandering in his direction. He was way too handsome, possessing those Black Irish good looks that formed a criminally sexy combination. Jet black hair and magnetic blue eyes, and once you threw that rock-hard body into the mix, you got one delicious looking male.

Tonight he was wearing all black again, snug pants that hugged the curve of his ass and a T-shirt that couldn't hide the rippled muscles of his chest if it tried. His roped forearms flexed enticingly as he slid a couple of strawberry daiquiris in front of two female customers, and the crooked grin he flashed them sent a spiral of heat through Darcy's body.

Damn it. Like the dumbass she apparently was, she'd gone and opened Pandora's sex box, and now she couldn't close the stupid thing. X-rated images sizzled through her mind, all of them involving Reed's muscular body in various states of undress, which only caused a dose of guilt to join the desire coursing in her veins.

He was AJ's best friend, for Pete's sake. She wasn't allowed to harbor such wicked thoughts about him.

In an attempt to distract herself, Darcy sipped her Coke and eavesdropped on the conversation of the two women beside her. They were in their early twenties, both decked out in skintight dresses and impossibly high heels. Their heads were huddled together as they spoke in raised voices over the pounding music.

Initially, Darcy thought they were discussing a phone call with a guy that one of the girls was crushing on, but after a couple of minutes, it became evident they were talking about something entirely different. The person whose call they were waiting for wasn't a boyfriend or a crush—it was a drug dealer.

"No," the blonde was saying, "we don't have to go anywhere. He sells it right here at Sin."

Darcy froze, the hairs at the back of her neck standing on edge. AJ had mentioned that a drug dealer was using the club as his headquarters, but they hadn't figured out who it was yet.

"How did you even get his number?" the other girl asked.

"Mac gave it to me. But he warned me that this guy is

totally on the down low. Everything is super hush-hush, but his stuff is good and he sells it cheap." The young woman glanced at her phone display, then squealed. "Ooh, he just got back to me. Come on, let's go. You have cash on you, right?"

As both girls hopped off their stools, Darcy sprang to action, lightly touching the blonde's arm. "Excuse me."

"Yeah?" The girl eyed her warily.

"I didn't mean to eavesdrop—I swear, I don't usually do that—but...Do you think I could get that phone number from you?" Darcy put on her most innocent, unassuming face.

Suspicious brown eyes peered back at her. "Why?"

She offered a sheepish smile. "I've been trying to score some—" she leaned in to whisper into the woman's ear "—Ecstasy for weeks now, but my usual guy is dry."

"Really? You don't look like the type who, uh, uses that stuff."

Darcy laughed. "I don't do it often, but every now and then I feel like getting a little...*happy*, if you know what I mean."

The two women giggled. "Oh, we definitely know what you mean," the brunette answered.

The blonde quickly clicked a couple of buttons on her BlackBerry, then turned it around so Darcy could view the screen. "Here. Hope this helps you feel happy tonight." She shot her a warning look. "But you're only allowed to text him. He won't pick up the phone if you call."

Darcy wasted no time pulling her own phone out of her purse and punching in the phone number. Once she was done, she winked at the two girls, thanked them, and then watched them scurry off and get swallowed by the crowd.

The instant they were gone, Darcy spun around and waved her hand in an attempt to get Reed's attention.

When he noticed her frantic movements, a slight frown marred his lips.

"Get over here!" she called.

Without an ounce of enthusiasm, he made his way over, wiping his hands on a red-and-white-checkered dishrag. "Hey, I know I'm taking a while, but I can't leave until my relief shows up. It's insanely busy tonight." He looked frazzled. "Normally we don't get a rush this big until closer to ten."

She spoke in an urgent tone. "I think I just found your drug dealer."

Confusion filled his eyes. "What are you talking about?"

"AJ told me there's some guy dealing drugs at Sin. Well, I just spoke to two girls who know him." Darcy beamed at him. "They gave me his phone number."

He gave a sharp intake of breath. "You're shitting me."

"Nope. It's right here on my phone. Should I text him?"

Reed's expression went deadly serious. "Yeah. Do it now. Tell him you're interested in buying a few party favors and you've got the cash."

Darcy started to key in the message, then stopped and shot Reed a blank look. "How do I phrase it? What does Ecstasy even come in? Hits? Pills? Fingers, you know, like whiskey?"

A laugh burst out of his mouth. "Yes, Darcy, ask for two *fingers* of E. Makes you sound like a real pro."

She scowled. "Excuuuuuse me for not being super knowledgeable about drugs and all the forms they come in."

"I thought you *knew* stuff," he said smugly.

Her scowl deepened. "Yeah, normal, everyday stuff. I'm not part of a drug cartel!" She pressed *send,* then set her phone down on the counter. "There. I kept it vague, so we should be good. Hopefully he texts me ba—"

Her iPhone buzzed before she could finish the sentence. Wow. That was one on-the-ball drug dealer. The kids in her eighth grade class could take a lesson or two from him about punctuality.

She quickly read the message, then relayed it to Reed. "He says thirty bucks for two pills—is that a reasonable price or should I try to barter with him?"

Reed rumbled with laughter again. "Tell him it's fine."

With a nod, Darcy sent an answering message, and just like before, a response came in right away, instructing her to go to one of the curtained-off alcoves situated throughout the club in exactly thirty minutes. She shot back a quick "KK" before grinning at Reed. "This is so exciting. I feel like a narc."

He snickered. "You watch too many cop shows."

"Yeah, well, you don't watch *enough* cop shows, otherwise you'd find this as exciting as I do."

A stern look sharpened his features. "It's not supposed to be exciting, Darce. Drugs are serious shit."

An annoyed shout sliced through the trance beat blasting from the DJ platform. "Yo, dude! Quit getting your mack on and bring us our beers!"

"I'll be right back." Looking unenthused, Reed hurried off to take care of the waiting patrons.

He didn't end up coming back for another twenty minutes, and Darcy was thoroughly impressed as she watched him move up and down the bar with ease, filling endless orders and flashing that cocky grin to every customer, male or female. At one point, he clicked on his earpiece and muttered something she couldn't make out, and then he was suddenly heading back to her.

He lifted up the wooden barrier that blocked off the bar area, opening his mouth to address her just as a tall, bulky man with a shaved head stalked up to them. Darcy recognized him as one of the bouncers, but she couldn't remember his name.

"What's up, boss?" the behemoth said brusquely.

"Jeff. Hey. You tended bar back in the day, right?"

The bouncer nodded. "Yeah…"

"Good. I need you to man the fort until Henry or Sue get here," Reed replied. "I've got something I need to take care of."

The bouncer's dark eyes shifted from Reed to Darcy, then back to Reed. "Everything okay?"

Reed leaned in and murmured something in the other man's ear. Darcy wasn't certain, but she thought she heard the words "our little problem" and "keep an eye out, seven o'clock" but Reed ushered her away before she could ask him what he'd said.

"So how are we doing this?" She had to bring her lips close to his ear, and his intoxicating scent immediately grabbed hold of her senses and stole her ability to think properly. She held her breath so she wouldn't have to breathe him in, once again reminding herself that she had no business thinking about how good he smelled. Or how yummy his ass looked in his black trousers.

"Not sure yet. We'll just wing it."

His cavalier response didn't surprise her. Reed had always come off as the kind of man who didn't put much thought behind his actions.

They traveled along the edge of the dance floor toward the other side of the cavernous room. Sin had an open-concept design—exposed beams all around the main floor, a bar spanning one side and tables lining the other walls, and a spiral staircase leading to the second-floor VIP lounge that overlooked the club. Tucked in various points of the club were little alcoves sectioned off with blood-red velvet curtains. Some of them contained plush loveseats for customers who wanted to take a breather in privacy, but according to AJ, most people ducked into those hidden nooks to fool around.

The alcove where the dealer had directed her didn't have any furniture. It was nothing but a dark, cramped space. Standing room only, which placed her in perilously close proximity to Reed.

There were ten minutes left in their allotted thirty, but Darcy wasn't ready to raise the subject she'd come here to discuss. Her hands had gone clammy, her pulse racing as she and Reed squeezed into the tight space. She wondered if a few of the walls in there were sound-proofed, because the music from the club sounded muffled in the alcove, making it much easier to hear each other.

"What are you going to do when he shows up?" she asked.

The flashes of light streaming in from the slight gap in the curtain highlighted the deadly expression on Reed's face. "I don't know yet."

"Bullshit. You're totally planning on roughing him up, aren't you?"

When he shrugged, his shoulder jostled hers, and the heat of his body seared her bare skin. Her heart beat even faster.

"Maybe," Reed said in a vague tone. "Depends on how agreeable he is." He paused. "But if I ask you to leave, please don't argue with me, okay?"

She wasn't sure she liked the idea of Reed getting violent with anyone, even a lowly drug dealer, but she was discovering that arguing with Reed was about as effective as trying to teach a dog to speak French. Total waste of time.

"So…school starts soon, huh?" His expression was tinged with awkwardness, as if making small talk wasn't his forte.

Darcy nodded. "Next week."

"Are you looking forward to it?"

"Definitely. I already started all my prep work last week. Setting up my classroom, going over the curriculum. Plus a lot of boring meetings, but I've gotten pretty good at secretly playing Candy Crush while Principal Donnelly babbles on about budgets and rules of conduct."

Reed chuckled.

"I'm dying to see my students again." She glanced over

with a smile. "I teach eighth-grade homeroom and English for grades six to eight, so a lot of my seventh graders from history last year will be in my homeroom this year. I'm excited."

"AJ said you're really good with kids." His voice turned gruff. "That's a damn good skill to have. A lot of folks don't know how to relate to kids."

"Oh, I love them." She grinned. "It helps that most of the girls watch all the same shows I do. Last year we held a weekly *American Idol* discussion group after school."

He cringed. "You're into all that reality show crap? I'm disappointed in you, Darce."

She was quick to voice a defensive protest. "I have a thing for Keith Urban, okay? So sue me."

Reed's head tipped to the side. "Keith Urban, huh? Is that your type then, Australian cowboys?"

"Naah, he's just pretty to look at."

He made a disapproving noise with his tongue. "Ha, and people accuse men of objectifying *women*. But you ladies are way worse, and you know it."

"Yeah, we're pretty terrible," she confessed. "I can't deny that."

Chuckling again, Reed checked the black tactical watch strapped to his wrist. He was one of the only men she knew who still wore a watch. Most people, herself included, just checked their phones these days.

"It's been thirty minutes," Reed told her.

Darcy shifted her gaze to the curtain, half expecting the dealer to pop through it at that exact moment. His text replies had come so fast, she figured he'd arrive at the proposed time on the dot, but it quickly became obvious that Mr. Drugs wasn't as reliable as she'd thought.

She and Reed chatted about nothing in particular for the next five minutes, but the dealer still hadn't appeared. When another five minutes passed, Reed cursed under his breath.

"I don't think he's going to show."

Darcy chewed on her bottom lip. "Why not?"

Rather than answer, Reed clicked his earpiece on. "Jeff," he barked. "Is anyone heading in this direction?"

She couldn't hear the bouncer's reply, but whatever it was, Reed didn't like it. He touched his ear, then glanced at Darcy and swore again. "I bet he was watching us the whole time and saw me come in here with you. He must know I own this place."

"That's kind of a leap. Maybe something just came up."

"From what I've gleaned, he's a sharp businessman. I don't think he would bail on a deal." Reed sighed. "I think this is a bust. Come on, let's go."

He reached for the curtain, but Darcy grasped his arm to stop him. And boy, touching him was a *big* mistake. His biceps were perfectly sculpted, his flesh hot and smooth beneath her palm. Her pulse instantly sped up, mouth going so dry it felt like someone had stuffed it with sand.

"Right," Reed mumbled. "You wanted to talk." His lack of enthusiasm didn't do much for her ego.

Darcy swallowed to bring moisture to her arid mouth. "Actually, I wanted *you* to talk. Last night…" She gulped again. "Last night you said that you have to act like a jerk towards me because it's the only way for you to…" She eyed him sternly. "Finish that sentence, Reed. To *what*?"

Reluctance dug a deep groove into his forehead. "It's nothing. Forget I ever said it."

"I *can't* forget. It's been bugging me all day. I need to know what you meant by that."

"It doesn't matter." Sounding frustrated, he gently uncurled her fingers from his arm. "Nothing good can come out of this conversation, baby."

Darcy frowned. "Don't *baby* me. And PS? I never took you for a coward. You've always struck me as a man who says exactly what's on his mind."

Something hot and dangerous moved through his eyes. "Why are you pushing this?"

"Because I'm curious."

"Curious? No, I don't think that's it." His voice was silky now, deep and mocking. He eased closer, his arm brushing hers as he shifted so they were facing each other. "This is more than curiosity. You're blushing. You know what that tells me?"

Her breathing went shallow. "What?"

"It tells me you know *exactly* what I meant last night."

"I…" Her next words were barely over a whisper. "I need to hear you say it."

Her body grew tight and achy as she searched his face, waiting for an answer. God, why *was* she pushing him? He was right, nothing good could come of this. Nothing good at all.

"Don't do this." A warning note crept into his husky voice. "Don't make me say it."

Darcy's heart was no longer beating at double time. It had skipped right over triple and was now veering into cardiac arrest territory. The air in the alcove became stifling, rippling with the tension she'd only begun to notice last night. And now it was impossible to ignore.

Reed was standing so damn close to her. Close enough that his addictive scent was once again wreaking havoc on her senses. Close enough that all she had to do was lean in slightly and their lips would be touching.

"You're right," she stammered. "You shouldn't say it."

"I shouldn't." Yet even as he voiced his agreement, his hand had risen to her face, his thumb delicately sweeping over her bottom lip.

Her breath hitched. God. Her entire world had reduced to this one moment, this one man. Her lips were actually trembling from the crazy urge to kiss him.

"Fuck." The expletive tore out of Reed's throat, his frustration thick between them. "I want you, Darcy. *I. Fucking. Want. You.*"

Shock slammed into her, along with a burst of arousal that seized her core. Oh God. She couldn't believe he'd said it. Couldn't believe she'd *pushed* him to.

Because now there was no way to *un*hear those blunt words. No turning back from them.

"Is that what you wanted to hear?" he said angrily. "I've wanted you forever. Every goddamn time I see you, I've had to force myself not to blurt it out. I can barely even *look* at you, for chrissake, because I'm scared you'll see it in my eyes. Is *that* what you want to hear?"

The confession sizzled through her body like merciless flames ravaging a dry forest. Her thighs clenched, breasts tingled, heart stopped. She wanted to dive through the curtain and pretend she'd never seen the raw lust in his eyes, never heard those gruff, honest words tumble out of his mouth.

But she was rooted in place.

They stared at each other for what felt like an eternity, neither one speaking. Darcy had stopped breathing a while ago, and now her lungs burned, almost as painfully as the desire burning in her blood. Reed's hand was still on her face, his calloused fingertips tracing the edge of her jaw. Her skin felt tight and prickly, the flames traveling south and tingling between her legs.

Reed's blue eyes blazed with accusation. "Why are you still here?" he burst out. "*Go*, Darcy. Just go."

"No," she whispered.

He took another step closer, crowding her, his broad body dominating every inch of the tiny space. Their mouths were so close she could feel his warm breath fanning over her lips, mingling with the sudden rush of air that seeped out of her lungs.

"You have to go."

She swallowed. "No."

"This is wrong." Half mumble, half moan. The anguish in his voice matching her own.

He cupped her cheeks with both hands, groaning when their eyes locked again. "Just once," he muttered. "I just need to know."

Her voice wobbled. "Know what?"

"What it would feel like." A determined glint lit his gorgeous eyes. "Maybe it won't be as good as I imagined."

A laugh shook out. "It might be awful," she said helpfully.

He groaned again. "Worse than awful."

"We'll probably hate it so much that—"

Reed's mouth crashed down on hers before she could finish.

And there was nothing awful about it.

She moaned the moment their lips touched, but Reed swallowed the desperate sound with his mouth. His hands landed on her hips to pull her closer, and he didn't even try to hide his erection. He simply thrust it against her pelvis and rotated his hips so she could feel every hard inch of him.

Darcy parted her lips, but his tongue didn't seek entrance. His lips teased hers with soft, sweet kisses that made her head spin and her body ache. He didn't seem interested in driving the kiss to a whole new level, and when she pressed her palms against his chest and felt the tension seizing his muscles, she realized he was purposely holding back.

With an agonized whimper, she sank her teeth into his lower lip, making her frustration clear. He cursed in pain, and she took advantage of his parted lips by slipping her tongue into his mouth.

It was all the impetus he needed. Gone were the feather-light kisses. Gone was the restraint. Darcy gasped as he devoured her like a starving man, his hungry tongue turning the kiss from exploratory to downright dominating.

"Oh God," she moaned. "Don't ever stop kissing me."

Reed rumbled out a noise that was more animal than man, a deep growl that vibrated in her bones. There was something predatory about the way he backed her into the wall, his mouth glued to hers as he lifted one of her legs to his trim hips and ground his lower body against hers.

Darcy wrapped her arms around his neck and held on tight. Lord, what was happening to her? A tornado of sensation swirled through her body, traveling from erogenous zone to erogenous zone, eliciting shivers, tingles, a deep ache that made her clit swell. She'd never felt anything like it.

"Goddammit, Darcy," he hissed out.

He rubbed up against her, each stroke of his impressive erection causing the seam of her jeans to press into her throbbing sex. The telltale signs of orgasm were already beginning to surface, startling the hell out of her. Holy shit. She might actually come. From dry humping.

The fact that there wasn't even a door separating them from the masses in the club only thrilled her more. She felt hot and dizzy, helpless to control the unfamiliar sensations. The lightning bolts of lust, the painful throbbing of her clit.

What *was* this? How was this happening?

Reed's tongue slicked over hers in another greedy kiss as he thrust against her, his hips pistoning erratically. The baseline pulsating in the club served as a soundtrack for their frenzied grinding, their greedy kisses, their desperate moans.

And that's when it dawned on her. She knew what this was.

It was passion.

Darcy squeezed her eyes shut and lost herself in sensation. God, she wanted to come. She *needed* to come. Her hips rocked into Reed, frantically seeking relief.

But just as the pleasure mounted and her sex clenched in

anticipation, the delicious friction disappeared.

In the blink of an eye, Reed had stopped moving, abruptly tearing his mouth from hers.

"*No*," she cried out, agony ringing in her voice. "Please don't stop."

...

Please don't stop.

Sweetest, sexiest words he'd ever heard, and if they'd been uttered by anyone else, Reed would've kept going in a heartbeat. But this was Darcy.

AJ's Darcy.

She wasn't his, damn it. She could never be his.

Breathing hard, he took a hasty step back and averted his eyes. He couldn't catch even the slightest glimpse of the desire etched into her beautiful face. One look and he'd be a goner, and right now, at least one of them needed to show some restraint.

And clearly it wasn't going to be Darcy.

When he spoke, his voice was gravelly, as if he hadn't had a sip of water in weeks. "We can't do this, Darce."

"We already are," she said unhappily. "It's too late to stop. I don't *want* to stop."

Like the weak, sex-starved man he was, he couldn't resist meeting her eyes again.

And bad fuckin' idea.

Her parted lips, still glistening from his kiss, and the rosy flush on her cheeks totally robbed him of breath. Christ, his dick had never been harder. All it would take was a few more thrusts and he'd come in his pants like an inexperienced teenager.

Which seemed to be precisely what Darcy wanted.

The wicked temptress stepped closer and boldly palmed

the bulge in his pants. "I don't want to stop," she repeated.

She cupped his cock, and his eyes promptly rolled to the top of his head. "Oh sweet Jesus. Don't touch me. Don't tempt me."

Misery clung to her voice. "Please, Reed, don't make me go home like this. I'm aching. I'm…God, I *need* this."

The anguished plea snapped the last thread of his control. He couldn't think. Couldn't speak. He just released a wild growl and pushed her against the wall again. He shoved one leg between her thighs, his groin throbbing to the point of agony.

"*Damn* you," he hissed out.

She gasped when his mouth latched onto hers again. Reed's brain turned to mush as he kissed her. All he could concentrate on was the softness of her lips, her intoxicating taste, her sweet vanilla scent. One trembling hand cupped her firm ass to keep her tight against him, while the other drifted up to her chest so he could squeeze one full breast. Her tank top was enticingly thin, her bra even thinner, and he groaned when he felt the outline of her puckered nipple poking into his palm.

"I'm gonna come," he choked out. "Any second now. I can't stop it."

Darcy shuddered, her tortured moan heating the air between them. "Neither can I. I'm too close…I'm…*Oh!*"

Pure male satisfaction slammed into him as she cried out in bliss, shaking in his arms as she found release. Her orgasm triggered his own, the force of it nearly knocking him off his feet. He buried his face in her neck, inhaling the addictive fragrance of her shampoo as bone-melting pleasure pulsed inside him. Jets of release soaked his boxers, but still he kept moving, rubbing his cock against her, digging his fingers into her ass and breast.

It took him a while to remember how to make his brain

and limbs work. At least a full minute before he was coherent enough to unglue his lower body from hers. He leaned his forehead against hers, ragged puffs of air leaving his mouth and rustling her hair.

Darcy's eyes were huge. Swimming with confusion, amazement, and worst of all, anticipation for *more*.

"Stop looking at me like that," he wheezed. "We can't… this can't…damn it, we shouldn't have done that."

The guilt hit him hard and fast, like a flash flood bearing down on a village without warning.

He'd made out with his best friend's girl.

He'd *dry humped* her, for fuck's sake.

And he'd *climaxed*.

Jesus. Forget the fact that in order to get up to his office and change his pants he'd have to walk through the club with a wet stain on his jeans. He could endure that humiliation.

But fooling around with AJ's ex?

He would never, ever be able to come back from this.

"Reed," she started. Then her mouth closed, and the same paralyzing guilt he was currently feeling seized her pretty face. "Oh my God, you're right. We shouldn't have done that." Her breathing became unstable. "We're terrible people."

Although he wholeheartedly agreed with her about the sheer crappiness of their actions, he refused to let her take the blame for any of it.

"No," he said sharply. "This is on me. It's my fault."

Her eyes blazed. "No, it's not. We both did this." She stumbled to the side, effectively putting some much-needed distance between them. "I have to go. I shouldn't have come here tonight."

"Darcy—"

She dashed through the curtain like an Olympic sprinter, leaving him alone in the alcove.

Rather than chase after her, Reed sucked a rush of oxygen

into his lungs. Christ, AJ was going to kill him.

And yet his best friend's wrath would be nothing compared to the self-directed anger and loathing bubbling inside him right now.

A helpless groan slipped out of his mouth. There was no way to ignore the truth—he hadn't changed at all. Clearly he was still the same screw-up he'd always been. A man who acted on impulse, whose good judgment flew out the window the second he decided he wanted something, and to hell with the consequences.

But there *would* be consequences to what he'd done tonight. A whole lot of them.

And not the good kind.

Chapter Four

Four days later, Reed strode into Paddy's Corner Pub in the heart of Southie and reluctantly made his way to the booth where AJ was already seated.

By some miracle, he'd managed to put off this confrontation for days. It helped that Sin was closed on the first three days of the week, which meant not having to see AJ at work, but when his friend had called earlier and cashed in on Reed's offer to go for drinks, he'd had no choice but to say yes.

The pub was one of his favorites in the city, a total man cave with simple wooden booths, plenty of dartboards and pool tables, and blinking neon beer signs hanging on the walls. And luckily, every patron in the bar tonight was male. Reed had been worried that AJ might want to chat up some girls, but after his explosive encounter with Darcy this weekend, the thought of scoring a hook-up was about as appealing as dyeing his hair pink.

Though if AJ's drawn features and beach bum attire were any indication, the guy wasn't in a lady-killer mood tonight, either.

Reed raised a brow at his friend's threadbare T-shirt and ratty old jeans with an honest-to-God hole in the knee. AJ was usually a sharper dresser than that, and Reed couldn't stop himself from making a smartass remark. "Jeez. Are you wearing the latest designs from the hobo collection?"

AJ sighed. "Dude, I haven't done laundry in days. I'm scraping the bottom of the barrel here."

Keegan, the sole waiter at Paddy's, approached the booth. He was a former boxer with a full red beard and a crooked nose that had been broken at least a dozen times.

Reed had trained in the same gym as the man, and he greeted Keegan with a big grin, rolling his eyes at the two bottles of Guinness in the man's hands. "Keeg, how many times do I have to tell you? I'd rather drink sewer water."

"You're a disgrace to your people, Miller," Keegan retorted in his thick Irish brogue. Scowling, he set the bottles in front of the two men. "You don't get your pansy-ass Bud Lights until you finish your Guinness like good little boys. Hear me?"

Reed and AJ exchanged an amused look as the man ambled back to the bar. "Why do we keep coming back here?" Reed said dryly.

"Because it's awesome." AJ picked up his bottle. "Now be a good little boy and drink your Guinness."

Sighing, Reed forced himself to choke down a sip of the too-thick liquid. "So whatcha been up to?" he asked his friend. "You've had the past six days off. Must have been nice."

AJ shrugged. "I haven't done much. Just hung around at home. Played video games. What about you?"

I fooled around with your ex-girlfriend.

Reed bit back the words. Blurting it out like that was definitely not the way to do it. For days, he'd been practicing what he would say to AJ, but now that they were face-to-face, the confession got stuck in his throat.

He knew that the second it slipped out, it would be an invitation to get punched in the face. Which he deserved, because he was total pond scum. He deserved every hateful word AJ was going to hurl his way, every accusation, every act of violence. What he'd done was unforgivable, he knew that, and yet at the same time, he wanted to hold on to this friendship for as long as he could.

He didn't have any siblings, or even parents. Reed's only family had been his late Uncle Colin, who'd taken him in when he was four years old, after his mother had died in a car accident. His father, sadly, was some faceless man who'd had a one-night-stand with Reed's mom and took off long before she'd discovered she was pregnant. Reed didn't even know his name.

Colin had raised Reed best he could, but the man had always been more concerned with getting drunk than nurturing or supporting his nephew. As a result, Reed had learned to seek out that support elsewhere, but he hadn't truly found it until he'd met AJ.

And now, because he'd given in to temptation, he was about to lose one of the most important people in his life.

"So Gage said you almost caught our dealer," AJ spoke up, his green eyes serious.

"*Almost* being the operative word. The asshole was a no-show." He battled a rush of frustration. "But we'll figure something else out. I'm pretty sure we haven't seen the last of that creep."

AJ hesitated, running one long finger over the label of his Guinness bottle. "Gage also mentioned that Darcy was the one who got the dealer's number."

Every muscle in Reed's body tensed. "Yeah, she stopped by the club to..." God help him, but he couldn't stop the lie from flying out. "To talk to you, I guess."

Surprise washed over AJ's face. "Huh. Did she say what she wanted?"

"Naah, she didn't say anything."

Shit, he was going straight to hell. Probably ought to pack up his sunglasses and SPF 30 in preparation, because there was no avoiding his fate.

Just tell him. Man up already.

He opened his mouth, only to get interrupted by AJ's quiet curse. "Okay, enough. We don't have to tip-toe around it, all right?"

Reed froze, an uncharacteristic vise of panic squeezing his chest. "What do you mean?"

"Darcy and I broke up. It's really not a big deal, so please, stop treating me like I'm a cancer patient or something." AJ grumbled in displeasure and dragged a hand through his dark blond hair. "I know you think she dumped me, but I promise you, that's not how it went down."

Reed knew he'd kick himself later, but he still had to ask. "What happened then?"

"Chemistry happened. Or rather, lack thereof." AJ picked up his beer and drank nearly half of it in one long swig. "We got along so well—we had the friendship part down—but there was no spark. No excitement." He shrugged again. "We made a go of it, it didn't work out, and now it's over. Time to move on."

Reed might've bought the speech—*if* AJ's tone had contained even an iota of conviction. But his friend sounded so glum that he suspected AJ was just reciting a rehearsed line. As if he were trying to persuade *himself* that the breakup had been mutual.

"Anyway, I have a favor to ask." Another sip, and AJ had drained his beer. He slammed the bottle down and fixed Reed with a somber look. "I need you to help me out with Darcy."

The panic returned, winding around his spine and making

his skin go cold. Damn it. He couldn't let this continue. Three more seconds, and he might be forced into agreeing to play Cupid on a quest to bring AJ and Darcy back together.

And even though he was still racked with guilt over what he'd done, Reed felt sick to his stomach at the thought of Darcy and AJ rekindling the spark AJ claimed had been absent.

"Listen, man," he said roughly. "Before you say anything else, there's something I need to—"

"I know it's a lot to ask," AJ cut in, "but I feel like a total shit letting her down. I mean, I agreed to this months ago. But I think it would be too awkward to follow through."

Reed blinked. "Follow through on what?"

"I told Darcy I'd help her with this self-defense thing at her school." AJ's expression darkened. "You heard about that kid who was attacked in Dorchester at the beginning of the summer, right? The ten-year-old who was jumped by a group of teenagers for his allowance money?"

Reed nodded. He'd seen it on the news, and he'd been overcome with anger when he'd found out what those older boys had done to the poor kid.

"Well, that boy went to Darcy's school," AJ said grimly. "I don't think he was in any of her classes, but she knew who he was, and she was so damn upset when she heard what happened. I was over at her place a few days later and we came up with this idea to run a self-defense workshop for her eighth-graders. The school barely has enough money to keep the extracurricular activities going, so I offered to come in for free and go over some of the basics with the kids." AJ let out a breath. "I feel like a jackass for backing out, but I figured maybe you could take my place. The workshop is scheduled for the first week of school. Next Wednesday, I think."

Reluctance rose inside him, not because he didn't want to help out, but because agreeing to do so meant putting himself in close proximity to Darcy again. "Oh. I'm not sure if, uh…"

AJ frowned at him. "It's only a few hours of your time, man. One hour after school for three days. And the club doesn't open until seven, so it won't interfere with work."

One hour a day for three days? That was *three hours*. Three hours in Darcy's company, three hours of looking at her gorgeous face, three hours of fighting the urge to taste those sweet lips again.

God. He'd never survive it.

But what kind of heartless jerk said no to teaching a bunch of kids how to stay safe? Darcy taught at a public school in a low income, high crime area, where most of the students walked to and from school, crossing through some of the city's most dangerous neighborhoods. Knowing self-defense was imperative for those kids, and the fact that AJ and Darcy had come up with a plan to make that happen only confirmed what Reed had already known: the two of them were goddamn saints.

He stifled a sigh. Clearly this was a damned-if-he-did, damned-if-he-didn't situation.

"Sure," Reed said with nod. "I'd be happy to help out."

AJ looked pleased. "Thanks, man. Do you mind contacting Darcy to tell her about the switch? I can forward you her number right now."

Reed tried not to choke on the guilt as AJ picked up his phone and swiped his finger across the screen.

Damn it, what was the matter with him? The whole point of meeting AJ tonight had been to confess the truth, and instead, he'd agreed to place himself directly in the path of temptation again.

It was becoming glaringly obvious that he was a glutton for punishment. That seemed to be the only justification for all the screwed up decisions he was making lately.

Though if there was another explanation, he sure as hell

would love to hear it.

. . .

Girls' night was always a fun affair, but tonight, it was also a life preserver. Or maybe sanity preserver was a more accurate description. Ever since her thrilling, incredible, *immoral* encounter with Reed, Darcy had been caught up in a never-ending freak-out session, and she was in dire need of a distraction.

Since that night, she'd felt like she'd boarded a seesaw, alternating between bone-deep shame and uncontrollable longing. She'd almost called him a gazillion times demanding they do it again, except this time without a stitch of clothing acting as a barrier between them.

God, just *thinking* about him naked, imagining all those sculpted muscles pressed up against her, his powerful body crushing hers as his cock pumped inside her…it was enough to send a spike of desire straight into her core.

And, apparently, it was enough to bring her to countless self-induced orgasms, which she'd done frequently this week.

But whenever the urge to reach for her phone arose, she swiftly reminded herself that seeing Reed was *not* an option. Her breakup with AJ wasn't even a week old, and even if the two men weren't best friends, Reed Miller was the last candidate she'd consider for a relationship.

You could always take him for a fling, a naughty voice pointed out.

She immediately silenced the thought. Nope, couldn't do that, either.

Oh, and had she mentioned that Reed was *AJ's best friend?* What she and Reed had done was so wrong it ought to be illegal. What kind of woman threw herself at her ex-boyfriend's best friend like that?

And great, now she was slut shaming *herself*. Fun times.

"She's not paying attention to us."

The dry observation came from her friend Shannon, who taught art at Darcy's school. Since nearly half the teaching staff at Jefferson Middle School were in their mid to late twenties, Darcy was friends with most of her fellow teachers, and often hung out with them out of school hours. Tonight, though, only Shannon and Jayani had shown up to the Italian bistro where their weekly girls' night usually took place. It was Labor Day weekend, so everyone else was either busy or out of town.

Skyler Thompson, Gage's girlfriend, rounded out their little group. Darcy had hit it off with the younger woman from the moment they'd met, but the pretty brunette's presence tonight only reminded Darcy of Sin, which in turn reminded her of AJ, and from there, it didn't take long before her thoughts drifted right back to Reed.

"It's okay," Skyler spoke up with a laugh. "She gets a pass. Breakups suck."

Shannon's features softened as she looked at Darcy. "Are you doing okay, hon? You keep saying you're fine, but none of us will blame you if you want to cry a little."

Grinning, Jayani slid her linen napkin across the table. "Seriously, go for it. Maybe the waiter will comp our meals if you unleash the waterworks."

Darcy rolled her eyes. "Jay, if you want free food, just flash him that million-dollar smile of yours. That usually seems to work."

The stunning Indian woman didn't bother denying it. Jayani looked like she'd stepped off the set of a Bollywood movie, her features so flawless and exotic that she turned heads wherever she went. She was also six feet tall, which only added to her supermodel good looks.

Jayani batted her eyelashes. "It's not like I actively *try* to get free stuff. It just gets handed to me. What am I supposed to do, say no?"

Darcy and Shannon hooted, while Skyler giggled. Gage's girlfriend had joined them at girls' night enough times to have witnessed the way men looked at Jayani, and how easily she got her way without even having to ask.

"Oh, and to answer your question, I really am fine," Darcy told her friends.

"Really? You don't miss AJ at all?" Skyler hedged.

"I miss the friendship part," she admitted. "But the rest of it…God, this is going to sound horrible, but whenever AJ and I had sex, it was about as exciting as white rice."

She knew the picture she'd painted wasn't a pretty one, but it was the truth. Sex with AJ had been blander than bland. Hell, even kissing him had lacked excitement. AJ's kisses had been nice, but so very sedate.

Reed's kisses, on the other hand…

Nope, she wasn't allowed to think about those toe-curling kisses again.

Or the way he'd made her orgasm just by rubbing his thick erection against her fully clothed body.

"Well," Darcy said brightly, reaching for her menu. "Now that I've officially bummed everyone out, how about we order?"

Skyler snorted, then picked up her own menu. "Gage was so mopey that I was coming here tonight," she said as she scanned the entrée list. "He wanted to make me this new Thai recipe he got off the Internet."

"Jeez Louise. I can't believe you landed yourself a man who likes to cook." Envy dripped from Shannon's tone. "Tom would eat his own arm first before even thinking about preparing dinner." She was referring to her husband, who also worked at Jefferson as the Phys. Ed teacher.

Darcy loved watching Tom and Shannon together at

school. The couple fought like cats and dogs, but she had no doubt they loved each other. And with that kind of palpable passion, she suspected their sex life was hot enough to set their bed on fire.

Argh. Why couldn't *she* find a man who rocked her world like that?

You did. Saturday night.

Darcy smothered a groan. Jeez, would that inner voice just shut up already? Saturday night didn't count. *Reed* didn't count. She wanted to set fires with a man she'd actually be able to *keep*.

"Yeah, Gage is a real Martha Stewart in the kitchen." Skyler broke out in a grin. "But in the bedroom he's anything but." She paused. "Unless Martha is a secret porn star or something. In that case, he's like her in *all* areas of life."

Jayani picked up her glass of Merlot and took a dainty sip. "Boyfriends are overrated. Me, I'm having way too much fun playing the field to even *think* about settling down." She winked at Darcy. "Now we can play the field together. And you're in luck—I make a damn good wingman, if I do say so myself."

"I might take you up on that in the future, but right now I'm thinking I want to be alone for a bit, at least until I figure out what I really need from a relationship," Darcy said with a sigh.

Their regular waiter walked up to the table, greeting the four women with a smile. His dark eyes twinkled playfully as he gestured to their menus. "I don't know why you bother looking at those. You ladies always order the same thing."

He was right—none of them were very adventurous when it came to food. As every single woman ordered the exact same dish as last time, the dark-haired man laughed in delight, then wandered away without writing a single thing down.

Skyler leaned close and poked Darcy in the arm, her gaze fixed on their waiter's retreating back. "Why don't you ask Tony out? He's so cute. And he's single, right?"

She shrugged. "I don't know. Those slick Italian good looks don't do it for me. I like 'em a little more scruffy."

Skyler rolled her eyes. "Says the woman who was dating AJ. Doesn't get much more clean-cut than that."

"I know some scruffy guys," Jayani said helpfully. Then she made a face. "Most of them are total douche bags, though."

"It's not just the scruffy ones," Shannon said sadly. "If I had to hazard a guess, I'd say 50% of the male population is all douche."

Well, wasn't that a disheartening thought. Darcy knew the dating pool could get pretty grim, and now that she was single again, she wasn't looking forward to sifting through a whole lot of muddy water in search of that one sparkling diamond.

Crap. She was mixing metaphors again. Good thing none of her students were there to witness it.

"I guess it's good that I'm taking a break from men then," she said lightly. "Honestly, I'm looking forward to being on my own for a while."

"And hey, if you're ever feeling lonely, just pull Bob out of the drawer and put him to good use. You still have big green Bob, right?" Shannon teased, referring to the enormous vibrator Darcy had won as a door prize at Shannon's bachelorette party the previous year.

"Oh, I still have him." She decided not to mention that she'd used the toy more than once this week.

Or that she'd pretended it wasn't Big Green Bob who was fucking her senseless, but Reed Miller.

Okay, enough. She *really* needed to stop thinking about that man.

Except the universe clearly didn't *want* her to stop, because the second she banished his gorgeous face from her mind, her cell phone buzzed with an incoming text message.

From Reed.

She knew she shouldn't read it, but the temptation to do so was too darn strong. It lured her in like a siren's song.

Then again, was it the sirens' fault that all those sailors were too weak and stupid to resist it? So really, weakness and stupidity was what pushed her to swipe her finger over the screen.

The message was short and sweet: *Can I see u 2nite? Need 2 talk.*

Wow. She couldn't believe the request had come from him and not the other way around. Weren't women the ones who usually demanded to have the uncomfortable post-hookup talk?

But she knew she couldn't say no. The memory of fooling around with Reed had haunted her for days, gnawing at her like a dog trying to chew the last bit of marrow out of a bone. The sooner they spoke and put their transgression behind them, the sooner she could stop feeling like the worst human being on the planet.

Trying to be discreet, Darcy typed a short response, letting him know she was out but could see him afterward. They arranged to meet at the front stoop of her building, and after she'd tucked the phone away and lifted her head, she found her friends grinning at her.

"I thought you were taking a break from men," Skyler chided.

Darcy's cheeks grew warm, and she felt like strangling her English heritage for cursing her with a blush she could never hide. "Who says I was talking to a man?"

Shannon chortled. "You are the worst liar on the planet."

"Will you at least tell us his name?" Jayani teased.

Darcy averted her gaze, staring at the crisp white tablecloth as if it was the most fascinating thing she'd ever seen. "It's nobody. Trust me."

"Uh-huh," Shannon said in a singsong voice. "If you say so."

Fortunately, her friends didn't press for more details, and Skyler changed the subject to tell them about her first week at work. The younger woman had just finished her Masters and was now practicing under the supervision of a licensed psychologist, thrilled to finally be able to put her skills to good use.

Darcy was grateful for the reprieve, but although she made an effort to participate in the discussion, her mind was elsewhere.

With two short sentences, Reed had succeeded in ruining girls' night for her. Now, thanks to him, all she'd be able to think about for the next two hours was their impending meeting.

Chapter Five

Reed didn't get nervous often, but his hands were embarrassingly shaky as he parked his car at the curb a few steps from Darcy's building. Through the windshield, he saw her sitting on the bottom step of her stoop, the light fixture above her head bringing out the reddish highlights in her wavy hair.

He reluctantly slid out of the car and walked toward her, trying not to dwell on the appealing picture she made. Other than the night at the Krib, he'd never seen her in anything dressy. Usually she wore jeans and colorful tops, and he had to admit he preferred her casual style to the too fancy, too made up women he encountered at Sin on a nightly basis.

It was funny—before he'd met Darcy, he hadn't been drawn to the girl-next-door type. He'd preferred bold, confident woman who didn't mind taking a walk on the wild side. A nice rack didn't hurt, either.

Darcy was confident, sure, but she also radiated goodness. A sweet, compassionate side he tended to shy away from. But although she was sweet, she certainly wasn't *meek*. The woman challenged him like nobody ever had, and that only added to her appeal.

"Hey," he said gruffly, shoving his hands in his pockets. "Thanks for meeting me."

"Hey." She rose from her perch, her hands dangling awkwardly at her sides, one of them clutching a folded piece of paper.

"What's that?" he asked.

She glanced at the sheet as if she'd forgotten she was holding it. "Oh, just a memo from my landlord about some fire alarm and carbon monoxide inspection the building is doing next week. It was stuffed in my mailbox."

"Ah."

They both went quiet for a second.

"Um." Darcy fidgeted. "I'd invite you up, but…"

The smartass in him reared his annoying head. "But you're afraid if I come upstairs you'll end up ripping my clothes off?"

She rolled her eyes. "Well, aren't we arrogant?"

"Am I wrong?" He'd meant to voice the question lightly, just a little tease that meant nothing, but the words came out raspy and dead serious.

She faltered, averting her gaze for a beat before shifting it back to his. She looked utterly resigned. "I want to say yes, but I don't think you are. I never thought, not in a million years, that I'd be saying this, but…I've been picturing you naked ever since…" She trailed off, but they both knew what she was talking about.

Her honesty didn't surprise him. Darcy had been a straight shooter from the moment he'd met her. He got the feeling she always spoke her mind. Didn't avoid a single confrontation, no matter how uncomfortable it may be.

Normally he'd appreciate that, but learning that she'd been picturing him naked achieved the opposite result of what he'd come here for. He was supposed to tell her that what happened between them was a mistake. A mistake he didn't intend on making again. But then she'd gone and said the word *naked*, and now his mind was overflowing with the dirtiest, filthiest images known to man.

Reed cleared his throat, valiantly ignoring the merciless throbbing of his groin. "Look, I can't pretend I didn't enjoy what we did. I enjoyed it a hell of a lot. But…"

"But it can't happen again," she finished quietly.

"No, it can't."

"You know, you really didn't have to come all the way here for this. We could've had this talk over the phone." She sighed. "Is there a reason you decided to do it in person and up the awkward factor by a hundred percent?"

"That's not the only reason I came. I hate to break it to you, but things are about to get a little more awkward."

Suspicion clouded her eyes. "What do you mean?"

"I just saw AJ—" When she paled, he quickly held up his hand. "No, I didn't tell him. I was going to, but I didn't get the chance. He asked for a favor before I could."

"What kind of favor?" she said warily.

"He wants me to take his place at the self-defense workshop you guys are holding at your school next week."

A curse flew out of her mouth. "Oh crap. I totally forgot about that."

Pausing, she nibbled on her lower lip, and the cute nervous gesture sent a ripple of heat to his cock. He suddenly imagined those perfect white teeth nibbling on something other than her lip. His neck, for one. Or maybe his shoulder, so she could stifle a scream as she rode him to orgasm.

Christ.

Fantasies weren't usually his thing—good old-fashioned porn was enough to get him off—but his brain refused to quit running over all the delicious scenarios he and Darcy could find themselves in.

"I can see why AJ wants to back out." Sadness radiated from her petite frame. "But the workshop is so important."

"He feels that way too. That's why he asked me to do it." Reed swallowed. "Would you be okay with that?"

Her hesitation was palpable, but it didn't stop her from giving a quick nod. "We'll have to make it okay. The kids need this, especially after what happened to Jamal Littleton."

Reed shook his head in anger. "That poor kid. He's not still in the hospital, is he?"

"No, he got out last month."

"That's good." Reed stared down at his scuffed Timberlands. "Anyway, text me the details for the workshop. Dates, times, all that stuff. I'm happy to help out."

"Really?"

The skeptical note raised his hackles. "Why do you sound so surprised?"

"I don't know. You just don't strike me as the type of guy who's into community outreach."

Her answer only grated even more. "You think I'm not the type of guy who would want to help a bunch of children? Thanks for the vote of confidence, Darce."

Shame stabbed into him as he remembered that his first instinct at the bar the other night had been to say no to AJ's request, just for the selfish reason of avoiding Darcy. That she'd made the same assumption about his selfishness only heightened that feeling of remorse.

Clenching his teeth, he moved away from the stoop. "I should go. See you next week."

"Reed, wait." She grasped his forearm, her fingers warming his skin. "I'm sorry. I guess I had no right to say that. I don't know you well enough to make that sort of judgment."

"It's fine," he said roughly. "I really should go."

She paused, and then her voice went dry. "So that's it? Are we really not going to acknowledge the fact that we orgasmed together in a room the size of a closet?"

A burst of laughter flew out. "That's a nice way of phrasing it."

"How would you describe it?"

His gaze locked with hers. "I came in my pants dry humping you against a wall with my tongue down your throat."

Darcy gave a sharp intake of breath. "Yeah…you're right…my description *was* nicer. Yours just made me…"

This time when she drifted off, he truly had no idea what the rest of the sentence was. And God help him, but he wanted to know.

"My way made you what?" he said in a husky voice.

"Your way made me hot all over again."

Son of a bitch. Why, *why* had he asked? What was the matter with him that he kept giving in to self-torture?

A groan rose in his throat, but he choked it down. "You really can't say stuff like that. Not around me."

"Why not?" Her voice was barely above a whisper.

His frustration soared to a whole new level. This woman would be the death of him. He'd never experienced a craving this strong—even the last two times he'd tried to quit smoking had been a piece of cake compared to this. His hands itched with the need to explore every inch of her body. His lips ached to taste her.

Hot jolts of desire whipped through him, so powerful he was liable to burst into flames. His pants had become unbearably tight, his dick throbbing painfully against his zipper. He was nearing his breaking point, that critical moment of desperation where he either kissed the living daylights out of her, or ran far, far away from her.

The latter. Christ, he definitely needed to do the latter.

Unfortunately, Darcy seemed determined to push him to the limit. "Why can't I say any of that?" she repeated.

"Because I'm a selfish bastard. Damn it, Darcy, when a woman tells me I'm getting her hot, it just makes me want to prove how much *hotter* I can get her."

She moaned.

The goddamn temptress actually *moaned*, and the throaty sound sizzled into him and tingled in the tip of his cock. He was so hard he could barely breathe, and he wanted to shout at her to stop eyeing him like she was an addict and he was her fix.

"But I can't do that," he said helplessly, his voice strangled, tormented. "I can't do any of the things I want to do to you."

"Like what?" she murmured.

This time he was the one moaning. "I want to kiss you again. I want to bite on that sexy bottom lip of yours. I want to slip my tongue in your mouth and tease you until you're begging me to put my tongue somewhere else."

Her eyes went as wide as saucers, but he couldn't stop the wicked details that growled out of his mouth, couldn't censor himself even if he'd tried.

"I'd give you what you want, Darce. I'd lick my way down your body, and then I'd fuck you with my tongue."

"Oh *God*," she whimpered.

"I'd lick you for hours. I'd get you nice and wet and drive you crazy with my tongue, and then, when you're lying there limp with satisfaction, I'd crawl back up and fuck you with my cock until neither one of us can see straight."

His mouth snapped shut, breathing ragged as his explicit play-by-play came to an end.

Darcy's eyes had glazed over and her cheeks were so flushed he knew her body temperature must have skyrocketed.

Silence crashed between them. Long and deafening and simmering with sexual awareness.

"I should be offended and disgusted," she blurted out. "I should be angry at you for saying all those dirty things. But

I'm not." Something resembling defeat flashed in her eyes. "Come upstairs."

Surprise jolted through him. "What?"

"I'm inviting you upstairs, Reed."

There was no mistaking the lust in her eyes. Or the cloud of unhappiness.

"I know it's wrong. I *know* it. But maybe…" She bit her lip again. "Maybe we need to get it out of our system."

"We can't." It took every ounce of willpower he possessed to say those two words. "I can't do that to AJ."

"You already did," she said softly.

"Well, I can't do it again." Fighting a rush of regret, he took several steps back and did his best to ignore the insistent pleading of his impossibly hard cock. "You weren't there tonight, Darce. The guy is devastated over your breakup. If you and I hooked up, it would kill him."

She looked genuinely confused. "Neither of us was devastated by the breakup, Reed. It sucked, yeah, but we made the decision together."

"You didn't see him tonight," he insisted.

"You must have misinterpreted what you saw." Frustration filled her eyes. "I'm not saying he'd be thrilled if you and I… if we…" She didn't bother finishing the thought. "But it won't kill him. Eventually he'll come around to the idea of—" She stopped abruptly, and the dark look that swept over her face could only be described as self-loathing. "Oh, for fuck's sake! What am I even saying? Why am I pushing this?" She shoved both hands in her hair, her distress obvious. "For some reason I turn into a sex-crazed lunatic when I'm around you. What's *wrong* with me?"

He sighed. "It's lust. Regular old lust, and it will pass."

"Will it?"

Reed bit the inside of his cheek so hard he tasted blood in his mouth. "Yes."

He decided not to mention that this particular case of lust had been wreaking havoc on him for months. He ran his tongue over the tiny cut in his mouth, stepping even farther back, needing to put as much distance between them as humanly possible.

"We just need to forget Saturday night ever happened. It's the only way for us to move forward."

Darcy looked upset. "We should tell AJ."

"I'll take care of it," he said gruffly. "I'll tell him it was my fault, that I took advantage of you."

"But that's not the truth," she protested.

Reed exhaled slowly. "There's no reason for him to hate both of us, Darce."

"No. I can't let you do that. It's not right."

She sounded so distraught, he couldn't help but reach for her again. The hug was meant to be gentle and reassuring, but somehow turned into a desperate embrace that resulted in her face buried against his chest and his arms wrapped tightly around her slender body.

"Hey, it's okay." He was unable to resist stroking the small of her back. "We messed up, okay? Turned out there was an attraction there, and we gave in without thinking. I'll make sure AJ knows it was nothing but a random, stupid mistake, and that it won't ever happen again. Right?"

She tipped her head, those gorgeous blue eyes locking with his.

"Right?" he repeated, firmer this time.

It felt like forever before she responded with a slight nod. "Right."

Chapter Six

A week later, Reed was finally able to fully grasp the concept of irony. He'd been a professional fighter for ten years, won more matches than he could count, kicked more asses than he was proud of, and what did you know—he was actually nothing but a big, fat coward.

He'd had plenty of opportunities to tell AJ the truth over the past week…and he'd chickened out every damn time.

On the bright side, he was pretty sure he'd officially gotten over Darcy. Yep, he hadn't indulged in a single dirty fantasy about her for seven whole days. Hadn't even jerked off, which he deserved a goddamn medal of achievement for, seeing as how he hadn't gotten laid in almost three months. Thankfully, Sin had been busier than ever that weekend, and managing the club had distracted him from his unsatisfied libido.

He was confident that when he saw Darcy at the school, all the filthy, impure thoughts he'd once harbored about the woman wouldn't resurface.

He was wrong.

One look was all it took, one cautious smile from that

gorgeous mouth of hers, and not only did he spring a semi, but his mind was once again riddled with a week's worth of lustful fantasies.

"Hi." She greeted him on the front steps of Jefferson Middle School, wearing bright red shorts and a white tank top with the straps of a gray sports bra peeking out. Her hair was tied up in a high ponytail, giving her a youthful air that made him feel embarrassingly warm and fuzzy inside.

Reed managed a smile. "Hi."

"The kids are waiting in the gym," she told him. "They're wearing their Phys. Ed uniforms like you suggested. Oh, and we also set up the mats you asked for."

"Will any of the other teachers be joining us?" He held his breath, hoping she'd say yes.

To his disappointment, she shook her head. "I begged a bunch of them to help out, but it's amazing how many teachers refuse to be involved in extracurricular activities unless they absolutely have to."

They climbed the front steps, keeping three feet of distance between them as they headed into the school. Reed tried to walk at a brisk pace, eager to minimize the amount of time they spent alone, but he had no idea where he was going, so he was forced to match Darcy's easygoing strides.

Rather than bring a change of clothes, he'd decided to save time by showing up in boxing shorts and a wife beater, both black. When he noticed Darcy eyeing his bare arms and then glimpsed the resulting flush on her cheeks, he had to force himself not to make a flirtatious remark.

If she wanted to check out his guns, then fine. He, on the other hand, planned on keeping things strictly professional between them.

No matter how sexy she looked in her workout gear.

When they entered the gymnasium, Reed was instantly greeted by the sound of twenty or so loud, boisterous thirteen-year-olds. A dozen boys were zigzagging beneath the basketball hoop in a fast-paced game of pickup, while a group of girls congregated on the bleachers spanning one wall, whispering and giggling to each other.

Darcy clapped her hands to get everyone's attention, and suddenly those twenty or so pairs of eyes were wholly focused on Reed.

"Everyone head to the bleachers," Darcy called out.

Sneakers squeaked on the shiny floor as her students dutifully hurried across the gym to take their seats. Darcy and Reed walked over and stopped in front of the long stretch of blue mats that had been laid out on the floor.

"Guys, this is Reed Miller," Darcy said cheerfully. "He came here today to teach you—"

"How to kick butt," one of the boys yelled out, grinning widely.

She admonished the kid with a *look*. "To teach you self-defense. There will be no 'butt kicking' going on here today. Right, Kenny?"

Her student was suitably shame-faced. "Right, Ms. G."

Reed hid a smile. Man, he was totally digging the stern teacher thing she had going on. It reminded him of the crush he'd had on Mrs. Franklin, his ninth grade geography teacher. Holy hell, that woman's ass had been out of this world. He'd spent half his high school career admiring it, which probably contributed to the pathetically bad grades he'd brought home with every report card.

"Reed used to be a professional mixed martial arts fighter," Darcy informed the kids.

Several of the girls gasped, while all the guys looked thrilled. A skinny arm shot up in the air, belonging to an African-American boy with wild curly hair. He looked considerably younger than the others, and Reed wondered if he'd somehow wandered into the gym by accident.

But Darcy evidently knew him, because she smiled fondly at the boy and said, "Yes, Devon?"

"Did you ever knock somebody out?" the kid demanded.

Reed grinned despite himself. "Once or twice," he said vaguely.

Every male face in the gym looked impressed, while, as predicted, all the females gasped at his confession.

Darcy smiled at the kids. "As you can see, Reed is more than qualified to show us how to defend ourselves." She glanced over at him. "Why don't we start?"

He nodded, then addressed the group. "Okay, so before we get to the physical stuff, I want to make a couple things clear. I'm not sure if Dar—Ms. Grant went over this with you already, but the most important part of self-defense? Awareness." He put on a strict tone. "You need to be aware of your surroundings, guys. A lot of people wind up in trouble because they *place* themselves in dangerous situations that could have been avoided."

"We talked about that earlier today," Darcy told him before turning to her class. "Do you guys remember a few of the things we went over?"

A slender dark-haired girl spoke up. "Always walk in areas that are lit up."

Darcy nodded. "Yep."

Another girl chimed in. "Avoid taking shortcuts that lead you into alleys, or isolated places."

"Good. What else?"

Other kids started calling out tips.

"Don't go out alone at night, and if you do, travel with a group."

"Carry your cell phone if you have one."

"Tell people where you're going so they know where to find you if you don't come back."

"Don't talk to strangers."

"Stranger danger!" the runt—Devon—shouted in glee.

"Those are all very good strategies," Reed concurred. "But sometimes even the best prevention methods won't stop you from being attacked."

Every face in the gym clouded over with sadness, as if the kids were remembering what had happened to their classmate. The attack on Jamal Littleton had resulted in him being admitted to the hospital with a broken arm, dislocated jaw, fractured ribs, and two black eyes.

Reed was suddenly glad that he'd come here today. Seeing all their young innocent faces triggered his protective urges, and the thought of any of these kids getting beat up like their classmate made him all the more determined to show them how to protect themselves.

"We're going to start with something simple," he announced. "I like to call this technique the worm."

He was greeted with giggles.

"I know, it sounds dumb, but trust me, it's a good one. I'll need a volunteer, though." Although every hand in the gym flew up, Reed's gaze zeroed in on the smallest kid in the room. "Devon, my man, I think you might be just the guy for the job."

With an enormous grin, the young boy bounced off the bench and dashed over to the mats. Reed felt Darcy's eyes on him, and when he shot her a sideways glance, her smile nearly knocked him off his feet. Christ, she was so beautiful. *Too* beautiful.

He wrenched his gaze away, and cleared his throat. "Have you guys ever tried to hold a little kid who doesn't want to be held?" Reed asked the group.

That got him a chorus of yeses.

"You know how the kid responds, right? He wiggles around. He thrashes and squirms and bats at you with his hands, trying to weasel out of your grip. Well, that's what we're going to do now."

One of the boys groaned loudly. "We're going to wiggle around? That's no fun! I want to punch and kick someone."

Reed rolled his eyes. "Dude, I would love to see you punch and kick a man twice your size. Because trust me, most attackers *will* be twice your size. They'll cart you over their shoulders and you won't be able to do a damn thing about it. Except wiggle." His lips twitched. "But if it makes you feel better, I'll let you throw in some biting, scratching and gouging while you're wiggling."

The protester seemed appeased by that. "Cool. But you better teach us some real moves, too."

"Don't worry, by the time I'm finished with you guys, you'll have all the necessary skills to keep yourselves safe." Chuckling, he turned to shoot Darcy an apologetic look before adding, "And to kick a little butt."

• • •

Reed was good with kids.

No, Reed was *amazing* with kids.

Darcy couldn't believe her eyes as she watched him interact with her students. They'd graduated from wiggle strategies to more advanced moves, as Reed paired all the kids up. He was in the process of showing them how to target an assailant's most vulnerable areas, starting with the knee.

Darcy had worried that the workshop might get too violent, but Reed proved to be a natural teacher, as well as a cautious and intelligent one. He didn't allow too much physical contact between the kids, but the know-how and skills were still being transmitted.

A couple of times, he'd had to demonstrate a particular move on her, but his touch had been entirely impersonal. Nothing sexual about it, and yet her body tingled whenever he touched her. She'd attempted to hide her response to his nearness, and it helped that they were surrounded by children, but no matter how hard she tried, she couldn't stop her pulse from racing each time he wrapped one muscular arm around her or when his fingers grazed her bare arm as he showed the kids the best way to twist out of an opponent's grasp.

To make matters worse, her mind kept going over the text message she'd received from AJ earlier in the day. Even though she'd known Reed was planning on telling his best friend about them, she'd still been dreading AJ's reaction.

But her ex-boyfriend's message had shocked her to the core.

I hope it works out with Reed. He plays it like he's a tough guy, but he's got a good heart.

Um, *what*? Darcy had replayed the words in her head like a broken record, but unless she was missing something, there was really only one way to interpret them.

AJ had given them his blessing.

Which was *crazy*. Did he think she and Reed were dating now? Did he want them to?

Did *she* want to?

She couldn't deny she was attracted to Reed—and unbelievably tempted to explore that attraction—but sex and dating him were two very different things. She might be looking for passion, but successful relationships required a lot more than combustible chemistry. She wanted a reliable partner, a man who wasn't a "selfish bastard," as Reed had so readily described himself.

So no, she wasn't interested in dating a bad boy like Reed Miller. Never had been, never would be.

But sleeping with a bad boy? Well…maybe she could get on board with that, especially since AJ didn't seem to have a problem with it.

The workshop lasted an hour. The moment they wrapped

up, all the kids streamed into the locker rooms to change into their street clothes, while Reed and Darcy hung back to gather up the mats and stack them in the corner of the gymnasium.

"You were fantastic with them," Darcy confessed.

He looked embarrassed. "They're good kids. I had fun."

"I'm pretty sure Devon found himself a new hero." She laughed softly. "He was staring at you like you'd stepped off the pages of his favorite Superman comic."

"What's his deal anyway?" Reed asked curiously. "Did he skip a million grades or something?"

She shook her head. "He's a fifth grader. His mom doesn't finish work until five, and she doesn't want him walking home alone, so she has an arrangement with the school that Devon gets to sit in on whatever after-school activity is happening that day."

"Can't he take the school bus?" Reed asked as they headed for the double doors on the other side of the gym.

"Yes, but then he'd still be home alone until she got back. Their building isn't in the safest area, and Monique can't afford to pay for a babysitter. She's very protective of him."

"I don't blame her. He seems like a great kid."

They made their way back to the main lobby, pausing near the front doors. Although it wasn't part of her job description, Darcy liked to make sure her students were all right when they left the school after regular hours, and that the ones who were walking home were doing it in a group.

After the last kid had gone, she turned to Reed and said, "I just need to grab some things from my classroom. You don't have to stick around."

His blue eyes flickered with curiosity. "I wouldn't mind seeing your classroom."

She swallowed, unsure if it was a good idea for them to be alone for a second longer than they had to. He looked so damn good right now, in those long shorts that hugged his trim hips, and the tank top that outlined every curve of delicious musculature.

"Sure," she stammered. "It's on the second floor."

They ducked into the stairwell, climbing the steps until they reached the second floor landing. The brightly lit hallway was empty, all of its walls adorned with children's artwork and colorful projects stuck on Bristol boards. Darcy's key was attached to a spiral bracelet on her wrist, and she used it to quickly unlock the door to her classroom.

Reed's sharp gaze instantly swept over the room, taking in the neat row of desks, the wall of windows, and the blackboard covered with the grammar exercises she'd assigned for the first English class of the school year.

"I feel like I've traveled back in time." He wandered around the room, amazement clinging to his husky voice. Then he laughed softly, the rough masculine sound sending a shiver through her.

"What's so funny?" she asked.

"Ah, it's nothing." He turned to face her. "Did you get everything you need?"

Nodding, she held up her purse and the big stack of tests she was bringing home to grade. "Yep." She hesitated. "Would you be able to drop me off at home? I walked this morning, so I don't have my car."

"No problem," he said easily.

They left the school through the back doors, crossing the parking lot toward Reed's black Camaro. The drive to her apartment wasn't as tense or awkward as she thought it would be. They chatted about the workshop and what Reed planned on teaching the kids the following afternoon, and by the time they reached her building, she felt completely at ease.

At least until he asked if he could come upstairs.

"I'm dying of thirst," he said sheepishly, putting the car in park and killing the engine. "FYI—the water fountains at your school suck."

"Yeah, they tend to drizzle out drops instead of a steady stream," she answered with a laugh.

"Mind if I chug some water before I take off?"

She hesitated only for a beat. "Sure, come on up."

Her heart did flip after flip as they rode the elevator to her fourth floor apartment. She wasn't sure being alone in such close quarters with Reed was a good idea, but what was she supposed to do? Let the man die of dehydration?

Still, AJ's text message of blessing once again fluttered through her mind as she unlocked the door and gestured for Reed to come inside.

"Don't mind the teeny size of this place." She sighed. "It kind of grows on you after a while."

It was two steps from the front hall to the kitchen, and Darcy hurried to the sink to pour him a glass of water. "Want ice?" she offered.

"Naah, this is perfect. Thanks."

He drained half the water in one hearty gulp and she watched his strong throat muscles work as he swallowed. Once he finished, he went to fill up the glass again, chugged it as well, then glanced over and said, "So do I get the grand tour?"

She snickered. "Uh-huh. Sure." She moved to the doorway and pointed to their right. "Living room." Pointed to the left. "Bedroom and bathroom." She faced him again. "The end."

Reed chuckled as they drifted into the living room, which was just big enough to accommodate her sofa, coffee table, and TV unit, and a cramped office area in the corner with a large desk and two mini file cabinets.

"You're right," he remarked. "This *is* tiny. I'm surprised you don't get claustrophobic in here."

"Like I said, it grows on you." She wandered over to the desk and set the stack of tests next to the computer keyboard.

The sight of the sleek work surface reminded her of Reed's cryptic laughter in her classroom, and as usual, her curiosity got the best of her. "What were you giggling about when you were looking around my classroom earlier?"

He rolled his eyes. "First off, I'm a man. Men don't *giggle*."

"Mmm-hmmm. Whatever you say."

"I *laughed* because being there brought back some memories. I'm pretty sure the last time I was in a classroom, I was failing a test. Either that, or daydreaming about my geography teacher."

She stuck out her tongue. "He must have been a real looker."

"Ha ha. And I'll have you know, *she* totally was." A dreamy sigh escaped his mouth. "I would've cut off my right arm for a shot with Mrs. Franklin. Lord, she used to sit up on her desk, and she'd always wear the most indecently short skirts, flashing a helluva lot of thigh. I guarantee that every single boy in her class was trying to hide a boner with his geography book."

Darcy laughed. "Poor Mrs. Franklin."

"Poor Mrs. Franklin?" he echoed. "No way. That broad was totally digging the attention. She wore high heels and miniskirts to teach a *geography* class—trust me, she knew exactly what she was doing to us poor boys."

"Now I'm picturing a total seductress. Like a Mrs. Robinson type." With a grin, Darcy sidled back to her desk and hopped up on the edge. She crossed her legs, then leaned back on one elbow, trying to strike her most provocative pose. "Is this how she'd sit?"

Uh-oh. Big mistake.

In the blink of an eye, Reed's expression had flooded with heat. The man even licked his lips, which summoned an instantaneous response from her. Her body tingled as his smoldering blue eyes seared right through her clothes and brought goose bumps to her skin.

Despite her better judgment, she dropped her gaze to his groin, and her breath lodged in her throat when she saw the outline of his erection straining beneath his shorts.

"You're just as bad as Mrs. Franklin," Reed said in an accusatory voice. "Get off that desk before I do something stupid, Darcy."

She swallowed the moisture that had filled her mouth. "What kind of fantasies did you have when you were sitting in her class?"

He growled. "You really don't want the answer to that."

I hope it works out with Reed.

AJ's words buzzed in the forefront of her brain again, bringing a rush of uncertainty. She was tempted to ask Reed exactly what AJ had said to him when he'd confessed, but at the moment, his sexy body was too big a distraction. So was the predatory gleam in his eyes as he advanced on her.

Her heart did a crazy flip, anticipation surging in her veins as she met his eyes.

"Tell me," she murmured. "Tell me what you imagined doing to her." She drew a deep breath. "Or better yet, show me."

Chapter Seven

Darcy held her breath as she waited for Reed to respond. His shoulders stiffened, but that didn't stop him from moving closer, until he stood only a foot away from her.

"I thought we agreed we weren't going down this road," he said hoarsely.

"Maybe I changed my mind," Darcy answered, her voice equally hoarse.

Unhappiness lurked in his eyes. "AJ—"

"AJ will be fine," she finished quietly. "He's a grown man, and I don't think he would appreciate us treating him like a fragile piece of china."

Taking another breath, she uncrossed her legs.

After one heart stopping moment, Reed eased in, slowly, deliberately, until he was fully cradled between her thighs. His erection pushed against her mound, the hard ridge making her wet, and then impossibly wetter when he rotated his hips.

"I want you so bad I can't think straight," he mumbled.

Darcy's hand trembled as she raised it to his strong jaw, lightly stroking the bristles dotting his face. His facial hair was more of a perpetual five o'clock shadow than a tidy beard, and she liked the way his stubble abraded her fingertips. She suddenly imagined it scraping her inner thighs when he buried his face between her legs, and an uncontrollable shiver skittered up her spine.

Reed sagged into her touch, his eyelids fluttering closed to reveal surprisingly thick lashes. God, he really was a beautiful man. Long limbs, heavy muscles, and chiseled features created the most tantalizing package she'd ever seen.

She'd noticed those good looks plenty of times before, but she'd never truly *admired* them. Now, with him inches away, she couldn't tear her gaze off him, couldn't stop her fingers from exploring every inch of his face.

"Just once," he said thickly. "This can only happen once."

Her head jerked in a nod. But even if she'd wanted to complain about his laying down the law, she didn't have time, because his head dipped down and suddenly he was kissing her.

Darcy was happy to be sitting down, otherwise the impact of that passionate kiss would have knocked her right over. Reed's tongue plunged through her parted lips, tangling with hers, and then he thrust one hand in her hair and angled her head to drive the kiss even deeper. Sexual excitement burned in the air, licked through her body in long, pulsing waves.

She couldn't resist touching him. Everywhere. Running her fingers up and down his chest, sliding her hands over his firm ass to give it a hard squeeze. He groaned and rocked his hips, each sensual thrust causing his cock to glide over her aching sex.

She needed more, damn it. She needed everything. And apparently so did he. His frantic hands tugged on her clothing, peeling her tank top and sports bra over her head, shoving her shorts and panties down her legs. His hurried movements knocked the stack of papers onto the living room floor and pushed the computer keyboard to the far end of the desk, where it teetered perilously close to the edge. She was naked now, while he remained clothed, but once again she didn't have time to protest the injustice.

Reed dropped to his knees in front of her, his warm palms braced on her thighs as he gently parted them. He sucked in a breath at the first sight of her most intimate place.

"Oh Jesus," he hissed out. "You don't know how long I've wanted to do this. How long I've wanted to put my tongue. Right. Here."

Darcy moaned when he made contact, licking a slow circle around her clit. *So* good. It felt so criminally good that stars flashed in her vision. She was worried she might actually pass out.

Reed's tongue followed the line of her slit to her opening, lapping up the evidence of her arousal. He groaned again, a husky humming sound, laced with such approval and joy that a desperate laugh flew out of her mouth.

"I didn't think guys got this much pleasure from going down on a woman," she choked out.

He tilted his head back, startling her with the intensity of his gaze. "Baby, I could eat your pussy for hours. I could make you come like this over and over again, and enjoy it just as much as I would if my cock was buried inside you."

"Is this what you wanted to do to Mrs. Franklin?" she said in a breathy voice.

"Yes." He stroked his thumb over her folds, his features taut with pleasure. "But not as badly as I've wanted to do it to you."

He lowered his head again, each deliberate lick tightening the knot of pressure forming in her core. Pleasure prickled over her flesh, throbbed in her clit, caused every muscle in her body to tense with anticipation.

"I want you to come," Reed muttered against her aching

flesh. "I want you to come on my face and my tongue, and scream my name while I drink you up."

God, she'd never been with a man who talked dirty. AJ hadn't, and neither had her previous boyfriends. It thrilled her. Probably more than it should, but holy moly, just hearing those X-rated words leave his mouth made her senses come alive.

She whimpered when his mouth closed over her clit. He sucked on the sensitized bud, softly, gently. *Too* gently. Darcy lifted her hips, trying to deepen the contact, desperate for relief.

Growling with approval, he sucked harder, one finger teasing her opening before plunging deep. With his finger pumping into her and his mouth and tongue devouring her clit, Darcy came with a wild cry of abandon. Shards of pleasure exploded inside her, rendering her speechless. Leaving her limp and breathless.

Reed rose with a satisfied chuckle. His hot mouth latched onto her neck, kissing and sucking her feverish flesh as he continued to fuck her with his fingers. Two now, then three, stretching her wide, curling over a spot deep inside and promptly reigniting the fire threatening to consume her.

She'd never come without clitoral stimulation, but whatever he was doing to her, that spot he was hitting...it unleashed a rush of ecstasy she wasn't prepared for. It wasn't an orgasm she was used to, less of an explosion and more of a slow burn, but *hot damn*, she certainly wasn't complaining.

"Hell, Darcy. You're so wet. So tight." He rumbled out the words as his fingers stilled, then withdrew from her core.

She felt empty without them, desperate for that feeling of completion again. "I need you to fuck me. Please, Reed, *please.*"

She didn't recognize her own voice. Didn't recognize herself. She was naked on her desk, for Pete's sake. Naked and begging to be fucked. But she didn't care how weak or needy that made her.

This was precisely what she'd craved—dirty, passionate sex that wasn't encumbered with common sense or propriety or the self-consciousness that usually hit her when she was intimate with a man.

Reed's chest rose and fell rapidly as he reached for the waistband of his shorts. Then his fingers hesitated. She could see his brain working through the implications, the consequences, but she didn't give him the chance to surrender to them. She reached out and shoved his shorts down his trim hips in one swift motion.

The first sight of his cock made her moan. It was long and hard and massively thick, a clear drop of arousal pooling at his engorged head. As her heart pounded like a jackhammer, she curled her fingers around his shaft and stroked him with her fist, eliciting a husky noise from his throat.

"I think I'm in love with your dick," she announced.

He croaked out a laugh. "That's incredibly forward of you. At least buy him dinner first. I'm curious, though. What did it for you? The length? The girth?"

A smile stretched across her mouth. "Naah, it was the thought of how good it's going to feel inside me."

A hiss shot out when her exploratory caresses turned into fast pumps. "Baby, if you keep jacking me off like that, you won't get the chance to experience it. I'm gonna come all over your hand."

As appealing as that sounded, she refused to deprive herself of the sensation of his hard cock pulsing inside her when he climaxed.

Releasing him, Darcy stretched one hand toward the arm of the couch where she'd left her purse. She swiped the leather bag by the strap and dragged it closer, then rifled inside until she located the small zippered pouch that housed her first aid travel kit. And her condoms. She was a grown woman living in the twenty-first century—condoms were a necessity.

Reed's expression turned reluctant as she proudly handed him the foil packet. "This still feels wrong."

A part of her agreed, but she couldn't derail the crazy train they'd boarded. Besides, she'd already experienced two mind-blowing orgasms. At this point, a third wouldn't make much of a difference.

Clearly Reed agreed. In a speedy motion, he peeled off his shirt, momentarily distracting her with his spectacular bare chest. Sleek golden skin and perfectly contoured muscles assaulted her vision. And oh God, he had tattoos. Several of them.

She ran her fingers over the black and red boxing gloves inked above his left pectoral, then traveled down to his hip, to the three rows of dates done in simple black calligraphy. She didn't ask what the dates meant. She was too distracted by the flash of green that caught her eye when he turned slightly. A lethal dragon spanning one side of his back, so vividly realistic that she shivered.

Reed rolled the condom on, his blue eyes smoldering as he stepped between her legs. Goose bumps broke out on her skin when he fisted his cock and rubbed the tip of it over her folds.

"I'm going to fuck you nice and slow," he rasped. "I'm going to make every second count, so neither one of us ever forgets how good it is."

Her entire body trembled with need, her legs widening on their own accord in anticipation of what was to come.

Reed's gaze stayed glued to hers as he dragged the head of his cock up and down her slit, taking his time, lazily bringing it to her entrance before gliding right back up. Neither of them spoke. Neither of them moved, except for his skillful hand on his cock, teasing her to oblivion.

Darcy had never wanted anyone so badly. She stared into his bottomless blue eyes, holding her breath, fighting the urge to beg again. She was so wet her juices now glistened on the condom, but still Reed held back.

His expression glittered with lust, the rugged planes of his face tight with passion. His tongue came out to moisten his bottom lip, his broad chest rising as he drew a breath.

Time stopped. So did the movement of his hand.

"Reed. Please," she whispered.

He made the sexiest sound she'd ever heard. Half growl, half moan, all man.

Ever so slowly, he guided his erection to her opening, then kept it there. He didn't slam in. Didn't thrust his hips. Only a fraction of an inch deep, a hint of what was to come.

Frustration seized Darcy's throat. Oh God. She might actually die if he wasn't inside her in the next three sec—

The loud knock on the door stopped Darcy's heart. Reed froze, his cock still poised millimeters from her core.

They stared at each other, rooted in place, utterly silent.

Another knock echoed through the living room. "Ms. Grant? Are you home? We're here to check your fire and CO detectors."

Oh crap. She'd forgotten all about that. Her landlord had specifically ordered everyone on her floor to be home today for the inspection.

She didn't answer, glancing at Reed in a panicked plea for help, but the evil gleam in his eyes told her he was the wrong person to ask.

A second later, he slammed his cock so deep she cried out in pleasure-laced shock.

Oh fuck.

Oh hell.

Oh fucking *hell*.

Reed was buried inside her, filling her completely.

And there were who knew how many fire inspectors standing right outside the door.

Her cry had clearly been heard because the male voice grew louder. "Ms. Grant?"

White dots swam in Darcy's field of vision as her inner muscles clamped around Reed's cock. The deep penetration and delicious stretch felt so damn good she couldn't move, let alone speak.

But she forced herself to respond to the worried inquiry. "Yes, I'm home," she called out in a wobbly voice. "I'm...here. In here. But I just got out of the—"

Reed eased his hips back, then drove inside her again.

"Shower!" she croaked. "I'm not...dressed...and—" her voice lowered to a hiss, "Oh God, don't stop. Please don't stop."

Reed didn't stop. Chuckling quietly, he thrust into her with long, hard strokes that made her vision go blurry again.

"Can you...check the other apartments first and then come back?" she practically wailed at the door. "I won't be long... I—"

Reed gripped her hips and started fucking her in earnest.

Darcy bit her lip to contain a moan. "I'm almost done—I mean, dressed! I'm getting dressed."

There was a beat, followed by a cheerful reply. "No problem. I'll start at the other end of the hall and make my way back to you."

She registered vague sounds—the soft thud of footsteps, low male voices in conversation, another knock from somewhere farther down the hall. But her attention was elsewhere. Every thought, every frantic heartbeat and ragged breath was focused wholly on Reed. His cock moving inside her, warm hands gripping her hips, sexy lips brushing her ear as he bent down to whisper into it.

"I promised you nice and slow, but circumstances have

changed. Hold on for the ride, baby."

Then those greedy lips captured hers in a kiss, and the rocking of his hips turned ferocious.

She came the moment his tongue touched hers. Choked on the blissful moans doing their damndest to slip out. She had to tear her mouth away from his, bringing it to his shoulder instead and biting his hot, male flesh to stop from vocalizing her pleasure. Reed grunted in pain, but he didn't slow down. The sound of flesh slapping against flesh echoed in the room with each furious thrust. His fingers dug into her waist, and the low groan he released told her he was close.

"Coming," he hissed out.

As his cock pulsed inside her and his shoulders shuddered from the force of his pleasure, Darcy was struck with realization. A clear, persistent truth she couldn't deny if she tried.

Once wasn't going to be enough.

Not by a longshot.

Chapter Eight

As Reed followed Darcy to the front door in silence, he snuck furtive glances at her, then kicked himself every damn time because her rosy glow and sated expression painted a picture of a woman who'd been well-sexed.

It only made him want her even more, but damn it, he wasn't allowed to. He'd given himself one free pass, thrown good judgment out the window and taken what he wanted. But he couldn't do it again. Sex with Darcy Grant was no longer on the table.

Darcy stopped at the door, her forehead creasing. "Now what?"

Reed puffed out a breath. "Now I go home."

"I see." Zero emotion in her voice, but he sensed her displeasure. "And then what?"

"And tomorrow afternoon, I'll be at the school for the second day of the workshop." He paused. "And tomorrow night, I'm going to talk to AJ."

"Talk to him about what?" she said in confusion.

He shot her a pointed look. "What do you think? I'm

going to own up to being a selfish son of a bitch and confess that I slept with his ex-girlfriend. And afterwards, I expect I'll be rewarded with a black eye, maybe two. Then again, AJ's a lot deadlier than he looks, so it could be much worse."

Darcy's bewilderment only seemed to get stronger. "But you already told him everything."

He frowned. "No, I didn't."

"But..." In the blink of an eye, she dashed to the living room and returned a moment later with her cell phone in hand. "He sent me this text earlier, and it totally sounded like he knew about us. You said you would tell him last week..."

"I say a lot of things," Reed muttered. "But I didn't tell him. I kept chickening out." He sighed. "Can I read the text?"

She handed him the phone without a word. Reed skimmed the message, then heaved out another sigh, this one weary as hell. "I think he was talking about the self-defense class, Darce. About the *workshop* working out, not you and me working out."

She was stricken. "Crap. Oh crap. I'm such an idiot." A strangled noise popped out of her mouth. "The only reason I let this happen was because I thought I had his approval."

Reed arched a brow. "That's the only reason?"

She slowly shook her head. "No, it wasn't just that. I wanted you. I won't pretend I didn't." Her throat dipped as she visibly swallowed. "I *still* want you."

His throat tightened. "I still want you, too."

The confession jerked his cock to attention, as if the big guy wanted to voice his agreement. Christ. Ten minutes ago, he'd come so hard he'd seen black spots, and his dick was still nowhere near satisfied.

The memories of Darcy's beautiful naked body flashed through his mind, taunting him. Her silky skin, endless curves, those perfect tits he'd barely even touched. There were still so many things he wanted to do to her, damn it. Flick his tongue over her pale pink nipples, lick the soft swells of her breasts, trail kisses along the flat expanse of her belly. And don't even get him started on everything he could do south of that delicious border.

"Look...we've already crossed the line," Darcy said miserably. "We might as well have a fling."

His stomach went rigid. "A fling," he echoed.

"Do you want to call it something else? A casual affair? A liaison?"

It didn't escape him that the word *relationship* hadn't made it on her synonym list, but then again, why would it? Reed knew what she thought of him. In Darcy's eyes, he was a player, a bad boy, a shallow, impulsive man she'd never dream of getting serious with.

His heart clenched at the discouraging thought. Fine, maybe he'd been that way once upon a time, but over the past few years he'd worked his ass off to break those old destructive habits.

When he'd first met Darcy, he hadn't taken one look at her and thought, *man, that's a chick I want to bone*. He'd known right away that the woman was special. Everything about her, from her contagious laughter to her sunny demeanor to the way she challenged him, had told him Darcy Grant was someone he could fall in love with.

But evidently *he* wasn't someone *she* could fall for.

Which hurt a lot more than he'd ever admit to her.

"So you just want to screw around with me for a while? A few days, a few weeks, maybe even a month?" It was difficult to curb the sarcasm dripping from his tone.

His heart only squeezed tighter when Darcy appeared genuinely confused by his hostility. "Are you saying you *don't* want to have sex with me again? Because you seemed pretty into it ten minutes ago."

How fucking perfect. It hadn't even occurred to her that

he might be interested in a relationship. In her mind, sex was all he was capable of wanting from someone.

But hell, why was he getting angry? It didn't matter what he wanted. Even if she *had* viewed him as a worthy partner, she was still AJ's ex-girlfriend. Any relationship they had would always be haunted by AJ. It'd be a never-ending spiral of guilt.

Sex, on the other hand, well, he was perfectly capable of performing *that* particular task, even when riddled with guilt. He'd get an ass kicking from AJ regardless, so why not experience a few more earth shattering orgasms with Darcy while he had the chance?

"You want a fling? Fine. I'll give you a fling," he said gruffly.

Her eyes narrowed. "You will?"

"Why not? You're right, we already crossed the line. We might as well keep being selfish and have some fun."

"What about AJ? Are you going to tell him?"

"I'll tell him when we're done having fun." If the guilt didn't eat him alive first. "I'm going to lose my best friend either way, so why not delay the inevitable?"

Sadness washed over her face. "So, what, we'll sneak around for a few weeks? You're going to see AJ at the club four nights a week and not say a word to him?" She gave the decisive shake of her head. "You're wrong. Losing him isn't inevitable, but it *will* be if you see me behind his back. We can't have a fling, Reed. Not unless we tell AJ."

Reed clenched his teeth. Damn it, she was right. He wouldn't be able to stomach it if he fooled around with Darcy on the sly. AJ deserved better than that. They all deserved better than that.

"All right. I'll talk to him tomorrow," Reed told her. "But depending on how the conversation goes, this fling you want might not work out."

"I can live with that." Her tone grew firm. "But AJ still needs to know."

Reed nodded sadly. "Yes. He does."

She nibbled on her lower lip again, a nervous habit he was growing accustomed to.

He couldn't believe they were standing around talking about coming clean to AJ and asking his permission to engage in casual sex. It was fuckin' ludicrous, and yet Reed had every intention of following through on it. Call him greedy, but he wanted to have his cake and eat it, too. He wanted to be honest with his best friend and find a way to keep AJ in his life.

But he also wanted Darcy.

He didn't care if he only had her for a month, or a week, or even a day. Now that he'd gotten a taste of her, he wanted more. He was dying to explore the sexual chemistry between them. And yes, he didn't need AJ's permission to do that, but he didn't feel right keeping secrets from his best friend.

"I'll see if he can meet up tonight," Reed said quietly. "If not, I'll tell him tomorrow." His gaze locked with hers. "The club closes at midnight during the week. Is that too late for you to see me?"

Uneasiness filled her eyes, along with the unmistakable gleam of anticipation. "No. It's not too late." Her voice was throaty.

"Even on a school night? You might be tired," he pointed out.

"How about you just call me, and I can tell you whether I'm too tired for you to fuck me." She let out a resigned sigh. "But I'm pretty sure the answer to that will never be *no*."

• • •

Rather than heat up leftovers for dinner, Darcy decided to

drop in on her mother. She was too wired to be alone at the moment and way too confused to be trusted with her own thoughts.

It didn't take long to reach her mother's house, a cute seventies-era rancher in the West Roxbury neighborhood. She pulled into the driveway and parked behind the blue pickup truck Carol Grant had been driving for years. Darcy rolled her eyes each time she saw the rusty old monstrosity. She'd pointed out to her mother on more than one occasion how much more difficult it was to maneuver the streets of Boston in the truck, but Carol refused to sell the pickup, no matter how many times her daughter tried to persuade her.

Darcy strolled into her childhood home without knocking and breathed in the familiar smell of pine cleaner and baked goods. The house had changed little in the forty or so years Carol had been living there. It boasted the same furniture, same wallpaper, even the same outdated kitchen counters.

Carol liked everything a certain way. She was predictable to the core and extremely averse to change, which was why Darcy always found it odd that her mom had married someone like Stuart Grant. Darcy's dad was the farthest thing from predictable. His every decision, his every action, was the direct result of a whim. Sure, he was also the most charming man she'd ever met in her life, but he definitely wasn't someone Darcy could rely on.

"Hey, Mom," Darcy said, poking her head into the living room.

Carol was on the flower-patterned couch, a pair of knitting needles in her hands and a ball of blue yarn on the cushion beside her. "Darcy!" The older woman looked thrilled to find her daughter in the doorway. "You didn't tell me you were coming by."

"It was spur of the moment. I decided your leftovers would probably make for a better dinner than mine." She sighed. "I swear, I follow all your recipes word for word, but my cooking never tastes half as good as yours."

Her mother grinned. "That's because you always forget the secret ingredient."

"If you say love again, I'm going to—"

"*Love*," her mother finished, beaming at her.

Darcy pretended to gag. "You're the cheesiest person on the planet."

"Yeah, but you still adore me."

She couldn't argue with that. She happened to adore her mother to death.

"I just need to finish up this row and then I'll meet you in the kitchen," Carol said, her deft fingers working the knitting needles with impressive speed. "Why don't you make us a salad? I can heat up some lasagna to go with it."

"Sounds good."

Darcy wandered into the incredibly out-of-date kitchen and began gathering up ingredients for a salad. As she sliced tomatoes at the counter, her mind drifted to Reed, going over every detail of the out-of-this-world sex they'd had less than an hour ago.

In her living room.

Right on the desk she worked at almost every evening.

God, how would she ever be able to sit behind that desk again without thinking about it? Without thinking about *him*, and how astonishingly good he'd made her feel?

What was even more astonishing was her suggestion that they have a fling. Darcy had never seen the appeal of casual sex. She loved all the things that came with relationships. The cuddling, the intimacy, sharing her feelings, having someone to talk to.

She and AJ had mastered all of that, but the physical aspect of relationships was just as important to her, and sadly, she and AJ had never really found their groove. Even their kissing had been boring.

Kissing Reed, on the other hand, was not the least bit boring. It was exhilarating, and when she was with him, she experienced the excitement she'd been longing for.

But she wasn't foolish enough to think he could offer anything more. In the five months she'd been with AJ, she hadn't seen Reed get serious about anyone. His life was an endless parade of women, and Darcy had no intention of getting her heart broken by the man.

"Okay, tell me what's on your mind." Her mother entered the kitchen and spoke in a no-nonsense tone.

Darcy glanced up from her dicing. "What makes you think I have something on my mind?"

Carol snorted. "Ha. You actually expect me to believe you stopped by just to raid my fridge? On a school night? I know you better than that, sweetie."

Great. Apparently she was equally predictable. "Fine, you caught me."

Smiling, Carol pulled a large Tupperware container from the fridge and set it on the counter, then grabbed two plates from the aging wood cabinet next to the sink. "So what's going on?"

Darcy was usually able to talk to her mom about anything, but sex wasn't one of the topics she brought up freely. Feeling a tad awkward, she chose her words carefully. "I'm thinking of doing something potentially stupid."

Carol sighed. "Is this another tattoo conversation? Because I already told you, I don't care if you get one. Just make sure it's not a butterfly at the small of your back. I was at the supermarket the other day and there was a woman about your age with one of those. I saw it when she bent over to get something from the bottom shelf. Oh, and her thong was peeking out of her jeans. It was horrifying."

Darcy burst out laughing. "Don't worry, I'm not planning

to get a tramp stamp."

"Is that what they're called? That's not a very nice term."

"No, it's not, but most of the slang these days isn't very nice." She bit her lip. "I'm considering having a casual…affair, I guess? Yeah, a casual affair."

Carol's eyes grew serious. "Well. You've gone out on casual dates before, no?"

"Dates, sure. But even if it's just a first date, I still go into it entertaining the possibility that it could lead to something more. With this, I know for a fact that it won't."

"Why do you say that?"

She paused, thinking about Reed's rough-around-the-edges personality. He'd already admitted to being impulsive, and she knew from AJ that he'd never had a serious relationship in his life.

"He's not really my type," Darcy admitted. "He's sort of a bad boy. Has a wild reputation, doesn't take things very seriously."

"Sounds a bit like your father."

She frowned, realizing her mother wasn't too far off base. Her dad was definitely impulsive, sweeping into her life a couple of times a year with his magnetic, larger-than-life personality. Darcy didn't think she'd ever had a meaningful conversation with the man.

"Is that why you and Dad got divorced?" she asked tentatively. "Because he was a bad boy?"

As usual, Carol's visible hesitation sparked her curiosity. Twenty-five years since the divorce, and Darcy still knew only the bare minimum of details about what led to it. Her mother had always insisted the marriage simply "hadn't worked out."

Today, however, Darcy found herself coaxing for more information. "I don't even know if you left Dad, or vice versa."

Carol released out a tired breath. "In the end, it was my decision. But your father didn't exactly challenge it."

With that, Carol refocused her attention on the lasagna, heaping two generous portions on their plates, then heating the first dish in the microwave. She kept her back to her daughter, but Darcy saw the tension lining her mother's slender shoulders.

"This wasn't something I ever wanted you to know," Carol said suddenly, "but I think it might be time you did."

The ominous remark made her gulp. Darcy put down her knife and watched as her mother slowly turned around to face her.

"Your father cheated on me."

Darcy's jaw fell open. "He did?"

"Oh, yes. He cheated quite a lot, in fact."

Waves of anger on her mother's behalf rippled through her chest. "I can't believe it."

Carol quickly held up a hand. "No, this is precisely what I didn't want to happen. I never wanted you to think less of him, or hate him. Stu hasn't been the greatest father, I'm the first to admit that, but he does love you, sweetie."

Yeah, he loved her enough to see her twice a year, three times tops. And he'd forgotten to call her on her birthday for the past four years in a row. He'd apologized for that, though, claiming he lost track of time when he was on the road. As a long haul trucker, Darcy's father spent ninety percent of his time driving across the country and doing God knew what in his spare time.

Scratch that—she supposed she now knew *exactly* what he did in his spare time.

"I can't believe you never told me. And why aren't you angry, damn it? You never, ever seem angry when you talk about him."

"That's because I'm not." Carol's features became drawn. "I'm sad. And I blame myself, partly."

"For *him* cheating on *you?*" Indignation boomed in her

voice.

"Sweetie, I knew what kind of man he was when I married him. I thought I could change him, and trust me, that's the worse mentality to have going into a relationship. You can't change people," Carol said sadly. "They are who they are, and yes, sometimes they do change for the better, but not because someone else made them. They have to decide to change for themselves, and your dad wasn't interested in doing that. He liked his freedom. He liked being on the road all the time. He told me that when we got married, and I lied and pretended to be okay with it because I was certain I could tame my bad boy."

Darcy bit her lip. "But you couldn't."

"No, and in the end, he resented me for trying to force him to settle down, and he broke my heart, just like I always knew he would." Carol moved closer and touched Darcy's cheek. "So my advice to you is, if you know that this man of yours isn't long-term material, then you need to make it clear going in. He needs to know what you want out of this affair before you start it."

"I kinda already made it clear."

"*Kinda* won't cut it, Darce," her mother said sternly. "There's no point in starting something you know will result in heartbreak. If you don't see a future with him, make sure he knows it. Sex can be fun, sex *is* fun, but it's not fair to lead him on, and you shouldn't get involved with him if secretly you have expectations about it leading to something more when you know it can't."

"I don't have any expectations." She felt herself blush. "I just want a little excitement for once in my life."

"And there's nothing wrong with that." Carol smiled. "If you want a casual affair, then have one. Just be honest about it from the start."

The microwave beeped, cutting off the discussion that

had become more serious than Darcy had intended.

"All right," her mother said brightly. "Now finish up that salad before the lasagna gets cold."

• • •

Reed found AJ in the walk-in cooler behind the bar, unloading a pallet of beer cases. Leaning his shoulder against the doorframe, Reed cleared his throat and said, "You have a minute?"

AJ's blond head lifted. "Sure. What's up?"

Reed stepped inside and closed the door, instantly enveloped by the chilly temperature in the cooler.

He'd come to work early just to have this conversation, since AJ had been too busy to meet up the previous night. Which meant that Reed's second workshop at Darcy's school earlier today had been pure torture. He'd promised himself he wouldn't touch her until he spoke to his friend, and by some miracle he'd managed to keep his hands off the woman.

"I need to tell you something," Reed started. Then he stopped. He took a breath, gathering his courage as AJ's green eyes watched him expectantly. "I did something pretty bad. Something you're not going to like."

AJ stiffened. "Yeah?"

He nodded. "I…" The confession shuddered out on a shaky exhale. "I slept with Darcy."

Dead silence crashed over the cold room.

Silence that went on and on and on, until Reed released a frustrated expletive.

"Did you hear what I said?"

"I heard you." AJ's voice didn't contain an ounce of emotion. Not even a twinge of anger.

Reed waited, knowing he should probably offer a more detailed explanation, feed his friend excuses, apologies, pleas, but his vocal cords refused to cooperate. He watched AJ's face, trying to make sense of that shuttered expression, but he truly had no idea what his best friend was thinking.

And he certainly didn't expect what AJ said next.

"Are you two dating now?"

Discomfort constricted his chest. "Ah…no. Not really. I mean, I…I wanted to talk to you first."

AJ nodded, then picked up the case of Bud Light he'd set on the floor. He heaved it on the counter and proceeded to pull longnecks out of the crate. Keeping his back to Reed the entire time. "I can't say I'm very surprised."

Well, that made one of them. Because Reed was downright shocked.

"That's it? You're not going to kick my ass to next week?" He let out an incredulous curse. "I slept with your ex-girlfriend, man. We both know I deserve a beating for that."

AJ glanced over with a wry look. "We both know you've wanted to do it for months. I guess I should commend you for at least waiting until we were broken up before you made a move."

Bile coated his throat. He choked it down, wondering if the suffocating guilt would ever go away. His friend's impassive tone was like a knife to the heart. He would have preferred anger or accusations or a deadly right hook to the jaw. He wanted to shout at AJ to put down those damn bottles and come at him. God knew he'd deserve it.

"Jesus, Reed. Stop looking like your dog just died. Darcy and I are over. There's no reason why the two of you can't go out." AJ's light remark was too confusing to fathom.

And totally misguided, because Darcy didn't *want* to go out with him. She wanted a fling and nothing more, which she'd reiterated to him when they'd parted ways at the school earlier.

Reed was no stranger to flings. He knew all about them,

knew exactly how to maintain an appropriate distance, how to stop himself from revealing too much to the woman in his bed, how to keep her from thinking they could have something more than good old-fashioned fucking.

But he wasn't sure he could do any of that with Darcy. Not when he'd been infatuated with her from the moment he'd laid eyes on her.

"I don't understand why you're not mad," he said quietly.

For the first time since Reed had dropped his bomb, AJ conveyed some genuine emotion: annoyance.

"First off, would it make a difference if I was? Won't change the fact that you slept with her, or that you're planning on doing it again. So really, all I can do is accept the news like a grown-up."

He swallowed a lump of self-loathing. "You're a better man than me, then."

AJ put down the beer bottle in his hand and shot Reed a resigned look. "Besides, you and Darcy make a lot more sense than she and I did."

He blinked in surprise. "We do?"

"Yeah." AJ shrugged. "A woman like her might be good for you. Someone sweet but strong, someone who won't let you get away with any bullshit."

Reed was absolutely floored. He'd always known AJ was the greatest person on the planet, but this went beyond that. This was...selflessness personified.

"I honestly don't know what to say," he said roughly.

"You don't have to say anything." In the next beat, AJ's eyes took on an ominous light. "But you do need to know something else."

Reed gulped.

"I still consider Darcy a good friend of mine. She's an amazing woman, and she deserves a lot more than what you usually give women," AJ said in a grave tone. "She's not someone you can fuck and then discard."

The indictment hurt. Reed couldn't deny he'd played the field, but Christ, he'd never *discarded* anyone. The women he'd been with usually shared his mindset. They'd wanted no-strings sex, a temporary arrangement that gave both sides what they wanted before they parted ways.

When AJ noticed Reed's upset expression, he cursed softly. "Sorry, that came out wrong. I know you're not like that."

"Well, it doesn't matter, anyway," he muttered. "She's not interested in anything serious with me. Just a fling."

AJ wrinkled his brow. "She told you that?"

"Loud and clear."

"That's weird. Darcy's not a fling girl. I wonder why—"

"You *know* why," Reed interrupted bitterly. "Because she thinks I'm a screw-up. I'm just a guy to pass the time with between the sheets, not someone she'd actually have a relationship with." When AJ didn't answer, Reed couldn't help but bristle. "I guess you agree with her, then."

"No. Not entirely. But you can't deny that you don't exactly have a good track record with relationships. Or with acting responsibly."

Familiar feelings of remorse and inadequacy washed over him, triggering another jolt of bitterness. "You know, for someone who keeps saying how much I've changed, I'm not sure you really believe it."

His friend met his hard gaze head on. "No, I'm not sure *you* believe it. You're not the same man you were a few years ago—I can totally see it. But I don't think *you* see it. Or maybe it's that you don't trust it. I don't know. I'm not going to psychoanalyze you, Reed." AJ sighed. "If you want more than a fling with Darcy, then prove to her that you're not the screw-up she thinks you are. Either way, if you're going to get involved with her, you need to treat her right. She deserves to be treated like a goddamn princess. She deserves... Everything."

Hell, just when he thought things couldn't get any more uncomfortable. Hearing AJ talk about Darcy like that only set off another bout of guilt.

"I won't see her again. Just say the word." Utter conviction rang in his voice. He meant what he'd said. He would gladly step aside if AJ asked him to.

But his friend shook his head. "I'm not saying *I'm* the one who wants to give her everything. Darcy and I are over."

Reed groaned. "This is fucking ridiculous. We shouldn't be standing around talking about this. Talking about her like she's some kind of commodity to be traded between us." He ran a hand through his hair, feeling like tearing it out by the roots. "I won't see her again."

Sighing, AJ went back to the counter. "I'm cool with it, okay? I'm not one of those assholes who subscribe to the whole 'if I can't have her, no one else can.' Like I said, treat her right, and we won't have a problem."

Reed was torn. A part of him wanted to be a good friend and promise AJ he wouldn't start something up with Darcy, but past experience proved that he had no willpower when it came to the woman.

God help him, but he wanted her again. Again and again and again. If he promised not to see her, he wasn't confident he'd be able to stick to that, and then he and AJ would be having this conversation all over again.

Except next time fists would most definitely be involved.

So he simply nodded and said, "I'll treat her right."

"Good." Without glancing over, AJ reached for another crate. "Just remember, I know where to find you if you don't."

Chapter Nine

It was a little past midnight when Darcy opened the door to let Reed into her apartment, and she didn't have to be a genius to figure out he was upset.

Especially since the first thing he said to her was, "I really shouldn't have come."

Darcy already knew he'd told AJ the truth earlier, not just because Reed had given her the heads up, but because AJ had called her himself an hour ago.

To her shock, her ex-boyfriend had actually given her his blessing. They'd even agreed to meet the following evening to talk about it more, an appointment that was made a gazillion times more awkward because Reed had texted right after she'd hung up with AJ, asking if he could come over after work.

She'd never been in a situation like this before. Wanting someone so desperately, while at the same time knowing what a terrible idea it was to open that door. Her conversation with her mother had helped ease some of her concerns, but Reed's unhappy expression quickly brought all of them back.

"This still feels wrong," he admitted. "Even though AJ knows, it still feels wrong."

"I know," she murmured.

Defeat flickered in his eyes. "I'm just... damn it, I'm gonna go."

Darcy nodded.

He nodded back.

Their gazes locked.

A split second later, they charged at each other, their mouths meeting in a hungry kiss that summoned simultaneous groans. Darcy clutched the front of his T-shirt to keep from keeling over with pleasure. She'd wanted to kiss him all day. The urge had nearly suffocated her as she'd spent an hour after school watching his powerful body showcase the self-defense moves he was teaching her kids.

Now that she was finally in his arms again, with his wicked tongue in her mouth and his firm body pressed up against her, she didn't ever want to stop.

"I'm addicted to you," he hissed into her lips. His hands slipped down to cup her ass, squeezing hard enough to make her gasp. "Tell me to go, damn it."

"I can't." She heard the helpless note in her voice. "I want you too much."

She grabbed the back of his head to bring his mouth down to hers again. She wasn't usually so aggressive, but something about Reed unleashed this desperate, starved side of her. Everything about him turned her on.

His kiss set her body on fire, that talented tongue exploring every crevice of her mouth as if he couldn't get enough of her. She felt feverish and mindless as she wrapped her arms around his neck and shamelessly rubbed her breasts on his chest. Her nipples puckered from the friction, tingling uncontrollably.

"Reed." His name left her mouth in a breathy rush. "I

don't want you to go."

"I don't want me to go, either," he said huskily.

Not another word was spoken as he scooped her into his arms and marched over to the living room couch. She almost pointed out that her bedroom was less than ten steps away, but at the moment, ten steps felt like a three-mile trek through the Grand Canyon. She needed him *now*.

Darcy clawed at his T-shirt, peeling it off his torso to reveal his mouth-watering chest. His hands had gone for her shirt too, ripping it off in one frantic move. The rest of their clothes didn't stay on for long.

Naked, they fell back on the couch, Darcy's butt bouncing on the plush cushions.

"You're so beautiful." Absolute reverence clung to his voice as those blue eyes roamed every inch of her body.

Everywhere he looked, she burned. Her breasts became hot and achy, her clit swelled with need, and the pressure between her legs grew so unbearable she started to squirm.

"So beautiful," he murmured again. "I want to fuck your brains out, baby."

She couldn't fight a wave of laughter. Only Reed would follow up a romantic compliment with something so colorfully crude.

She had to admit, she loved it. Fucking. *Loved*. It.

The dirty talk, the scruff on his face, the heavy cock that rested on her belly and left a streak of moisture on her skin when he shifted.

His beard growth scraped her skin as he slid lower, his warm mouth zeroing in on one breast. The second his lips closed over her nipple, her hips shot off the couch. A bolt of heat coursed from her breast straight to her clit.

Reed sucked on the distended bud, making the sexiest noise she'd ever heard. "I haven't paid nearly enough attention to your breasts. They're so insanely perfect. So damn sexy."

"Yeah?" She'd never paid much attention to her breasts, either. If she were being honest, she was much prouder of her ass.

"Oh yeah," he rumbled, flicking his tongue over her nipple. "These breasts deserve to be worshipped."

"Hmmm. Then maybe you need to quit talking so much and start worshipping."

His head lifted, one dark eyebrow propping up. "You really want me to shut up, Darce? 'Cause it seems to me that you totally get off when I talk dirty to you."

She pretended to think it over. "I guess I don't mind *some* conversation. As long as you shut up every now and then and put that filthy mouth to good use."

"Like this, you mean?" He drew her other nipple in his mouth and sucked so hard she cried out.

"God. Yes. Just like that."

Darcy clasped the back of his head to keep him in place, wiggling her lower body against his erection. Each soft lick and deep pull on her nipples intensified the ache in her core, and when Reed brought one hand to the juncture of her thighs, she knew he could feel just how wet his torturous ministrations had gotten her.

His lips released her nipple with a *pop* as he raised his head again. "Is this all for me?" he taunted, sliding two fingers into the moisture pooling at her opening.

She made a breathy sound. "Yes."

"How bad do you want my tongue down here?" His thumb slipped over her clit, stroking it lightly. "Tell me."

"So bad," she choked out. "So frickin' bad."

His chuckle was downright evil. "You want me to lick your pussy again? Like I did when you were sprawled on your desk, totally at my mercy?"

"*Yes.*"

She hadn't thought it was possible to be this turned

on. Her body actually hurt from the sharp prickles of need piercing her skin and the incessant rush of blood flow to her swollen clit.

"I've been thinking about it all day," Reed drawled, one hand lazily caressing her breasts while the other traced teeny circles over her clit. "Every time I see you I imagine burying my face between your legs. I picture you coming on my tongue."

"Do it. Please," Darcy pleaded.

She expected a mocking response, maybe even a denial, just because he seemed to enjoy tormenting her. But he simply hummed in approval and dragged his long, powerful body down to the end of the couch, his face inches from her core.

"Spread your legs wider," he ordered. "Let me see every inch of you."

She shamelessly did as he asked, offering him an indecent view. The intensity of his gaze made her pulse kick up a notch. So did the way he licked his lips, as if he were staring at a juicy feast he couldn't wait to devour.

The first swipe of his tongue was enough to send her eyes rolling to the top of her head. It was so damn good she could already feel the base of her spine tingling from impending orgasm.

Reed gave her another thorough lick, then another, nice and slow and so very sweet. She appreciated that he started off that way. Didn't apply too much pressure. Drew out her pleasure with the featherlight strokes of his tongue. This was a man who knew what he was doing, who gauged her responses and adjusted his technique based on each soft moan that left her mouth, each delighted gasp and sharp tug of her fingers in his hair.

"I..." Darcy fought for air. "I'm too close. I need...I need your mouth on my clit."

Groaning, he gave her exactly what she wanted. The moment he sucked, the pressure detonated in an orgasm that rocked her body and fragmented her mind. Darcy cried out when he slipped a finger inside her, pumping it in her wet channel to milk every last bit of pleasure out of her.

Her eyelids fluttered open once she'd crashed back to earth, and rather than feel lethargic or limp like she usually did after coming, every nerve ending in her body crackled to life and triggered a burst of energy that shot her up into a sitting position.

She jabbed a finger at him. "Get on your back. Now."

Humor danced in his eyes. "Someone's a little bossy."

"A lot bossy," she corrected. Her gaze landed on the erection jutting from his groin. "As of this moment, I'm in charge. So get on your back."

Jeez, where were these brazen orders coming from? She wasn't quite sure what had spurred them. All she knew was that she needed to explore every inch of this man's body. Make him come apart, the same way he made *her* come apart.

Reed didn't seem to be complaining. With a crooked grin, he stretched out on the sofa. His muscles flexed enticingly as he propped his hands behind his head and offered an expectant look. "There. Is this submissive enough for you?"

Her eyes never left his cock, which was practically beckoning her to touch it. "Oh yeah. That's exactly what I wanted."

Darcy scooted lower and straddled his knees, leaning forward to flatten her palms on his chest. His pecs quivered beneath her touch, telling her that he wasn't as relaxed as he was letting on.

She swiped her tongue over her bottom lip, then flashed him an impish smile. "You're not the only one, by the way."

His eyes narrowed. "The only one who what?"

"Who's thought about this." Her palm grazed his tight abs

before finding his cock. She slowly curled her fingers around the thick shaft. "I've also pictured you coming on my tongue."

Then she lowered her head and took him in her mouth.

• • •

Reed felt like he'd been poked with a cattle prod the second Darcy's lips enclosed his cock. His lower body jerked upward. The sensation of her hot mouth surrounding him was so intense he struggled not to prematurely blow his load and end things before they even got good.

And boy, did they get good. Darcy's mouth was pure heaven. Warm and wet and firm and—his brain swiftly blanked in the adjective department when she sucked him all the way down to the root, her happy little moan vibrating through his body.

"That feels so good," he mumbled. "Keep sucking me deep, just like that."

She licked a path along his shaft on the upstroke, then kissed the blunt tip before teasing the slit with her tongue and lapping up the moisture leaking out of it. Holy hell. He never wanted this to end. He never wanted her to stop.

Reed's fingers threaded through her wavy hair, but he didn't guide her head. He just stroked the silky strands as she gobbled him up with deep strokes and tight suction. Christ, he'd fantasized about this for months, but his meager imagination hadn't done it justice. He gazed down at the beautiful naked woman sucking his cock, floored by the sight, and more turned on than he'd ever been in his life.

"I love doing this." Her breath teased his engorged head, and then she began licking up and down his shaft like she was savoring a cool ice cream cone on a hot summer day.

Every sound she made brought on a violent shudder. He'd never witnessed a woman enjoying a blowjob this damn much, and he had a feeling that if he slipped his hand between her legs right now, he'd find her even wetter than before.

"Keep doing that," he groaned when her tongue found the sweet spot at the underside of his dick. Then she moved lower and he groaned louder. "Oh yeah, baby, use your tongue to play with my balls. Hell, that's good."

Her wicked mouth continued its torturous exploration, until his grip on her hair grew so tight he was scared he might be hurting her. But she didn't seem to mind. Her breathy moans echoed in the air, mingling with the wet sounds of her mouth devouring his cock.

Reed's pulse careened when she squeezed his sac, her lips wrapped firmly around his shaft as she increased the pace from fast to furious and propelled him to a whole new realm of mind-blowing pleasure.

"*Fuck*." As his balls drew up from impending release, he abruptly pulled out of her eager mouth. "I need to be inside you, Darce. I want to feel you squeezing my cock when I come."

She peered up at him with hazy eyes, and he'd honestly never seen a more beautiful sight. Her hair was tousled, cheeks flushed, lips glossy from sucking him.

Reed yanked her back in his lap, snapping one arm over the side of the couch in search of his jeans. His fingers collided with denim, frantically sliding into his pocket for the condoms he'd shoved there before he'd left the club.

Once he was sheathed, he gripped Darcy's slender hips and drew her down on his cock. The second their bodies were joined, his heart stopped beating and white dots flashed in front of his eyes. Sweet Jesus. Being inside this woman was the best feeling in the world.

She brought her mouth to his and he welcomed her kiss, his hips rising in an upward thrust as their lips met. Reed swallowed her moan of pleasure, kissing her so deeply his lungs were screaming for oxygen by the time he broke their mouths apart.

"Ride me hard," he ground out. "Take me straight to heaven, baby."

A faint smile lifted her lips. "I love having sex with you, Reedford."

"I'd be worried if you didn't, considering my cock is buried inside you right now." He chuckled. "Now are you going to fuck me or do I need to give you some incentive?"

She looked intrigued. "Hmmm. Like what?"

He placed his hand directly over her mound and dug the heel of it into her clit. A yelp flew out of her mouth, blue eyes instantly darkening with desire.

"That works," she said breathlessly, before raising herself up and then slamming down again.

Reed's pulse drummed between his ears as she rode him. Lord, her pussy was like a steel vise, clutching him so tight he didn't stand a chance in hell of restraining himself.

He came way too fast, and so hard his head slammed into the arm of the couch and his body went limp with mindless need. Hot waves of pleasure drowned out his thoughts, his surroundings fading away. Darcy was all he could concentrate on, and another shudder rolled through him when he felt her inner muscles spasm and heard her cry of release.

She collapsed on top of him, her firm breasts crushed against his chest. Reed's arms wrapped around her and stroked her back while she came down from the orgasmic high.

"You doing okay?" His voice was rusty thanks to his dry mouth.

Darcy responded with a sated mumble, her hair tickling his chin and bringing the sweet smell of her shampoo to his nostrils. He inhaled deeply, memorizing her scent, the way she felt in his arms.

The guilt he'd felt when he'd first entered her apartment didn't surface again. He was so content lying there with her, amazed that it was actually happening. He'd wanted this for so long. Long enough that his expectations could've easily been thwarted, the reality a disappointing contrast to his fantasies, but it was every bit as good as he'd imagined. No, it was *better* than he'd imagined.

Darcy gently eased herself off him. Her hair cascaded over one shoulder, so long that it covered her nipples.

He reached up and pushed those strawberry blond waves aside, his thumb and forefinger closing over one pink nipple to give it a teasing pinch. Immediately, heat flared in her eyes. She glanced down, sighing when she noticed that his cock was still semi-hard.

"Don't tell me you're ready to go again."

Reed grinned in challenge. "Don't tell me you're not."

"Dude, I'm a woman. Multiple orgasms, remember? I can go all night."

Damned if he didn't like the sound of that.

But her teasing expression quickly transformed into one of regret. "Actually, I can't. It must be one o'clock by now, which means I have to go to bed. My workdays start at eight in the morning."

"Right." Disappointment tightened his chest. He often forgot that not everybody started work at six p.m. like he did.

"Tomorrow is our last self-defense class," she reminded him.

"I know." He hesitated. "Maybe we can grab dinner afterward? You know, build our strength before all the wild sex we're gonna have."

She seemed equally hesitant. "I'm totally on board for the wild sex part. But, um, I'm not sure going out to dinner is a good idea."

Reed searched her face. "Why not?"

She proceeded to do that cute lip-biting thing again, an indisputable omen that he wasn't going to like what she had to say.

"I think..." Darcy sighed. "I think we both need to be clear about what this is."

"You wanted a fling. It's a fling." He couldn't stop the edge that crept into his voice.

"Yes, but we need to establish what each of us considers a fling." She nervously toyed with a strand of hair before tucking it behind her ear. "I don't want anything serious."

Reed bit his tongue before he could call bullshit.

But...*bullshit*.

Darcy Grant had *serious* written all over her, from the top of her head to the tips of her toes. Hell, she'd started referring to AJ as her "boyfriend" after two measly weeks of dating.

No, she didn't want anything serious with *him*.

That's what she'd really meant.

The notion made his gut clench.

"So you're saying there's no chance this will ever turn into a relationship?" he asked carefully, trying to mask his unhappiness.

"I don't see how it can," she confessed. "We're so different. And...well...I'll just say it. You're not really my type."

Annoyance streaked through him. "I get it. I'm good enough to screw, but not good enough to date?"

"It's not about being good enough," Darcy protested, misery etched into her face. "It's just...you really don't seem like a guy who's interested in relationships."

"You hardly know me," he said stiffly. "That's a rather big assumption to make, don't you think?"

"How many relationships have you been in?" she shot back. "And I don't mean flings or affairs or any other arrangements that revolve around sex. I'm talking about serious, long-term relationships. Commitments."

He supposed he could've lied, but he found it difficult to lie to Darcy. "Not a lot."

"How many?"

"None," he admitted.

Her forehead wrinkled. "None? Really? I figured you'd at least say one. What's the longest you've ever dated someone?"

"Never more than a month."

She nodded, as if it was just what she'd expected to hear. Although her expression didn't convey disapproval, he sensed it radiating from her body.

Reed could have elaborated. Explained how during his fighting days he'd been too immature to even think about commitment, too lazy to put in the effort required to make a relationship work. Or that lately, relationships hadn't interested him because he hadn't found anyone he truly clicked with.

But what was the point? She obviously had her own preconceived notions about his player status, but he suspected that even if he'd been living like a monk, Darcy Grant would still find him unworthy of the coveted boyfriend status. He was just a punk from Southie, a far cry from perfect, saintly guys like AJ, who clearly made up Darcy's "type."

Enough with the self-pity.

The angry voice in his head gave him pause. Yeah, he definitely needed to stop all this internal wallowing. He might've been a punk for most of his life, but damn it, he was trying to walk a different path now.

AJ had told him to prove to Darcy that he wasn't a screw-up anymore—evidently it was time to start proving.

"Look, I'm just trying to spare us from all the messy stuff that comes when people try to make things more serious than they are," Darcy said softly. "I think the best way for this to work is if it's a sex-only thing. No dinners or movie dates or heavy conversations about heavy topics." Her gaze probed his face. "Are you okay with that? Because if you're not, there's no point in going forward."

Was he okay with that?

Not fucking likely.

But he also wasn't an idiot. If he so much as hinted that he wanted something more, he knew she'd shut this fling down faster than a health inspector at a restaurant with a roach problem.

Maybe he and Darcy had a future, maybe they didn't. But he'd be damned if he didn't give himself the opportunity to find out.

So like an obedient schoolboy, he nodded and said, "Sounds good to me."

"Are you sure?"

"Positive."

He didn't miss the flicker of relief in her eyes. "Okay... well, good, then." She slid off the couch, distracting him with her naked body and the perfectly round ass she flashed as she bent over to pick up her clothes. "I'd offer to let you crash here, but I think sleepovers should be added to our *no* list."

"Naah, I get it. It's cool." Reed hopped to his feet, unfazed by his own nudity, then gave an exaggerated stretch because he knew damn well that it caused every muscle on his chest to flex.

As expected, Darcy's eyes glazed over as she stared at his body.

At least he had that going for him. The woman was wildly attracted to him, which was a damn good start.

As for her *no* list?

Well, he just happened to be a man who enjoyed a good challenge — and he had every intention of chipping away at Darcy's reluctance until he turned every last *no* into an eager, resounding *yes*.

Chapter Ten

The following evening, Darcy walked into Sin through the staff entrance she'd used dozens of times before when she'd visited AJ at work. Tonight, she was still there to see him, except this was the first time they'd be seeing each other as dreaded Ex-Boyfriend and Ex-Girlfriend.

She had steeled herself for what was bound to be an intensely awkward conversation, so when she entered his office and was greeted by a warm smile, her surprise was genuine.

"Hey, Darce." AJ rose from his desk chair and wasted no time striding toward her. The hug he gave her was sweet and familiar, and she found herself sinking into his embrace.

No matter how uneventful their sex life had been, she'd always loved AJ's hugs. He had a way of making her feel safe and protected, and she was glad to see that the warmth between them still existed even though they were no longer dating.

"Hey. How are you doing?" She pulled back to meet his eyes, her question laced with more than one meaning.

His green eyes glimmered knowingly. "Do you mean how am I doing with the breakup, or how am I doing with the fact that you're hooking up with my best friend?"

She winced. "AJ—"

He interrupted with a laugh. "I'm just being a brat, Darce. I'm fine on both counts."

"But *why*?" she couldn't help but blurt out. "Shouldn't you be yelling at me? I mean, most guys would *not* be cool about their ex-girlfriend turning around and sleeping with one of their closest friends. Which means you're either a saint, or a total dumbass."

"I'd wager a little bit of both."

AJ cast her the boyish grin that had charmed her off her feet the day they'd met when he'd approached her at a coffeehouse in Beacon Hill and informed her that she had the prettiest eyes he'd ever seen. They'd had coffee that day, dinner the following night, and within a week they were seeing each other exclusively. AJ was so damn easy to talk to, and so attentive to everyone else's needs, often sacrificing his own to make another person happy.

And now he was doing it again, stepping aside while she and Reed…did their thing, for lack of a better phrase.

"Honestly?" AJ said ruefully. "I can't say I was surprised when Reed told me what happened. He's usually good at keeping his cards close to the vest, but he did a pretty shitty job hiding that he had a thing for you. It was wicked obvious."

She blinked in surprise. "It was? Why didn't you ever tell me you thought that?"

"Because you were my girlfriend, *dumbass*." He rolled his eyes. "And at the time I still thought we might have something special. The last thing I wanted to do was plant the idea in your head and then watch you dump me for Reed."

"I never would have done that," she said firmly.

"I know. I just didn't want to risk it." He shrugged.

"But like my mom always says, the universe has a plan, and obviously it wanted you and Reed to get together."

"We're not together, per se. We're..." Her cheeks heated up. "I'm not really sure what we are. I honestly don't think it will go anywhere, though."

She figured it was wiser not to tell him that she knew for *certain* it wouldn't go anywhere—she planned on making sure of that. Taking her mother's advice, Darcy had plainly laid out the ground rules to Reed, and she was going to adhere to each and every one.

AJ obviously disagreed. "I think it will go somewhere, Darce. You and Reed make sense together in ways that you and I never did. I think it's the way you challenge him, and the excitement... That's what fuels a relationship. That's what we didn't have."

She smiled sadly. "But we had other things. Good things."

"We had friendship." With a smile of his own, he tweaked a strand of her hair before taking a step back. "Don't get me wrong, friendship is important too. But it can't be all there is."

He was right, but his quiet assertion still evoked a pang of sorrow. AJ Walsh was a standup guy. Sweet, funny, kind, supportive. Why couldn't she have fallen in love with him? He was the perfect man, for Pete's sake, and if the *perfect man* wasn't enough for her, then *who was*?

There was a knock on the door, and then Reed sauntered into the office. "Hey, man, do you—" He stopped short when he spotted Darcy. "Oh. Hi. I didn't know you were here."

"Uh. Yeah. I decided to stop by tonight instead of tomorrow. My friend Shannon has this improv show she wants me to go to tomorrow night, so I'll be busy...doing that..." She trailed off, her discomfort rising steadily.

It was so frickin' weird to share the same space as AJ and Reed, especially since she'd been in bed with the latter mere hours ago. The two of them had gone to her place after wrapping up the last self-defense class at her school, and just as she'd come to expect, the sex had been ridiculously awesome.

Now that Reed was five feet away from her, desire returned in full force, slamming into her like a sledgehammer. He was in all black again, wearing one of those tight T-shirts that hugged his broad chest, and pants just snug enough to outline his long, muscular legs.

And boy, it was *so* wrong to even acknowledge how sexy he was with AJ standing right beside her. A pretzel of guilt knotted around her insides as she looked from one man to the other.

"The improv thing sounds fun," Reed said lightly.

She fidgeted with the strap of her purse. "Yeah. Um. Should be a good time."

A brief silence fell over the room, broken up after a few seconds by AJ's exasperated sigh.

"Okay, I'll admit it—this is wicked awkward," he announced. "But you guys don't have to pretend you don't know each other. We're all adults here. I'm sure eventually things will go back to normal. Well, a new kind of normal, but normal all the same."

AJ was…extraordinary. Darcy couldn't think of another word to describe him at the moment. The man possessed the most uncanny ability to put everyone around him at ease.

Darcy leaned in and brushed a quick kiss on his clean-shaven cheek. "You're right. I'm sure we'll reach that normal point again. But I actually should get going. I don't want to bug you guys at work."

"I'll walk you downstairs," Reed said gruffly. He glanced at his friend. "I'll be back in a minute. Need to talk to you about that new liquor supplier."

"Sounds good," AJ replied as he headed back to his desk.

Darcy and Reed left the office, Reed pausing to close

the door behind them. The second they stepped into the corridor, a swell of muffled music from the club below met Darcy's ears, and the floor beneath her feet vibrated from the rhythmic bass line.

Neither of them spoke as they walked toward the staircase at the very end of the hall. The stairs overlooked a part of the club's main floor, and the music got even louder as they got closer.

Just before Darcy's foot hit the top step, Reed grabbed her hand and yanked her toward him.

His mouth crashed down on hers in a blistering kiss. Gasping, she flung her arms around his neck to steady herself and hungrily kissed him back. Their tongues tangled in a greedy duel, the heat of Reed's lips and his addictive taste snaking its way into her system until he was all she could see, hear, and feel.

Every time he kissed her felt like the first time. She wasn't sure she'd ever get used to the visceral burst of lust that erupted inside her whenever their lips met.

God, why couldn't she have found that level of passion with AJ? She suddenly had to wonder if that kind of relationship was even possible, the kind that combined all the wonderful things she'd had with AJ with the sheer passion she felt with Reed.

Reed's blue eyes glittered as he pulled back. "I wish you were naked right now."

Darcy's heart pounded as loud and fast as the dance beat blasting up at them. "Me, too."

"You sure I can't convince you to wait up for me tonight so I can see you after we close?" He slanted his head enticingly.

She shook hers. "There's no way I'll be able to stay up until three or four. It's only eight o'clock now and I'm pretty much ready for bed. Besides, I have some errands to run tomorrow morning."

He stuck out his chin, glum. "I hate weekends. By the time I leave this place, the whole world is asleep."

"How about this? Come over tomorrow night," she suggested. "I'll drink a ton of coffee during the day. That way I'll be wired and awake by the time you get there, and then we can sleep in because I have nothing to do on Sunday."

She realized what she'd done the second she finished talking—she'd invited him to spend the night at her place.

From the way his entire face brightened, he knew it too.

Crap. One day into their fling and she was already breaking one of the cardinal rules.

"Okay, I should get going," she told him. "I—" A flash of light in the corner of her eye had her turning her head, and when her brain registered what she'd glimpsed, her jaw dropped. She peered at the shadowy space dozens of feet below them, the strobe lighting making it incredibly difficult to see, but she was certain she hadn't imagined it. "Oh my God, Reed."

Concern creased his chiseled features. "What's wrong?"

"I swear I just saw..." She grabbed his hand and started tugging him down the stairs. "I think I know who your dealer is."

The music drowned out her last words, and Reed looked confused as he raised his voice and shouted, "You want me to feel *who*?"

"No, I know who the *drug dealer* is!" she shouted back.

Clearly he hadn't heard her again, because he still looked bewildered as she dragged his six-foot frame through the sweaty crowd.

Frustration hit her left and right with each body they had to dodge. She jostled one man, who spun around in annoyance and yelled something she couldn't make out, but his expression told her it had been nasty. With a hasty "sorry," she kept going, yanking on Reed's hand and hurrying all the way to the red curtain on the other side of the dance floor.

It was the same alcove where she and Reed had fooled around for the first time, but at the moment she was too tense to relive the naughty memory. She pointed at the curtain, then pinned Reed with an urgent look. "He's in there!"

Once again, the music overpowered her words, but Reed seemed to know exactly what she'd meant. His features hardened, broad shoulders stiffer than two-by-fours.

"Wait here." He stepped in front of her, gently moving her to the side before jerking aside the curtain and bounding into the alcove.

Darcy was too curious not to follow. She ducked in after him, blinking to let her eyes adjust to the darkness. When she spotted the two people huddled there, she gasped. She didn't recognize the skinny blonde in the tight top, but the man behind the curtain? It wasn't the Wizard of Oz, nor was it a little man pretending to be the Great and Powerful—it was Jeff, the bouncer she'd seen at the club dozens of times before.

"Son of a bitch." Reed sounded livid as he laid eyes on his employee, and then, when he glimpsed the small plastic baggie in the beefy man's hand, he cursed up a blue streak.

Jeff's face paled. "Reed, it's not what you—"

"Shut up," Reed snapped. He turned to glare at the female customer. "Get out of here. Now. Before I call the cops."

The girl scurried out of the alcove with such speed that Darcy couldn't help but be impressed.

Once she was gone, Reed directed that icy glare at the bouncer, his tone dripping with disgust as he took a menacing step forward. "Give me the bag, Jeff."

The other man was shorter than Reed, but had at least fifty pounds on his boss. Reed didn't seem deterred by that fact. When Jeff didn't hand over the drugs, Reed's arm shot out with lightning speed to snatch the baggie.

"Seriously? It was you all along?" Reed spat out. "All this

time you were pretending to help us find the dealer, and it was you? You goddamn son of a bitch. Do you realize that Sin could've been shut down over this?"

Jeff sputtered out a denial. "It's not what it looks like. I wasn't selling those, I swear. That chick is just a friend of mine and we were, uh, gonna get high together."

Reed's expression became incredulous. "One, that doesn't make this any fucking better, admitting you were about to get *high* on the job. And two? Bull-fucking-shit." He let out an angry curse. "I *vouched* for you! I asked Gage to hire you and this is how you repay me? By putting my job and everyone else's at risk?"

Reed suddenly looked stricken, sounding so betrayed that Darcy experienced a pang of sympathy. She hadn't realized he'd been the one to recommend Jeff for the security gig, and she couldn't imagine how awful he must feel knowing he'd allowed someone like that to work at the club.

With a lethal scowl, Reed clicked the earpiece Darcy hadn't even noticed he was wearing. "AJ," he barked. "Call Vinnie. I just found our asshole. And get Gage down here. The alcove near the emergency exit. It's one of our guys—"

Reed had barely finished his sentence when Jeff the bouncer slash drug dealer lunged at the doorway, trying to make his great escape.

He only made it two steps before Reed's fist slammed into the side of his face. The bouncer's head was thrown back from the impact, but rather than cower or surrender, a wild gleam entered his eyes and he went on the attack.

Darcy cried out when the man's meaty fist flew back at Reed. A sharp thwack and a grunt of pain sliced through the air, both sounds muffled thanks to the music pouring in from the narrow doorway. The alcove was too small to accommodate a violent fistfight, but that was precisely what the confrontation turned into.

Eyes wide, Darcy pressed her back against the wall as the two men came at each other in a blur of punches and jabs and undercuts that made her gasp each time knuckles collided with flesh.

"Reed, stop!" she yelled when he tackled the bouncer and slammed him into the wall.

Her voice temporarily distracted him, and Darcy cursed herself for opening her mouth, because it cost Reed his advantage.

Suddenly *he* was the one pinned to the wall, while Jeff's thick forearm rammed into his throat and elicited a choking sound from Reed as his windpipe was crushed in the powerful grip.

"Let him go, you stupid brute!"

Darcy hurtled forward without thinking and threw herself at Jeff. She collided into him with a thud, grabbing his hair with both hands and pulling hard.

The man roared in outrage, and then his elbow shot back and clipped her right in the face. She flew backward, promptly losing her footing and falling on the floor with an ungraceful thump.

The curtain suddenly whipped open, AJ's incensed voice rising over the music. "What the *hell*?"

Chapter Eleven

Reed struggled for air as his lungs began working again. AJ had yanked Jeff off him, and the bouncer was now being restrained by both AJ and Gage, who'd hurled themselves into the fray.

Panting out ragged breaths, Reed wildly searched the dark space for Darcy. His chest tightened right back up again when he spotted her on the ground.

Her palm was pressed to her left cheek, and the vulnerable, protective gesture smashed apart the last bit of his control. Growling, he threw himself at Jeff, whose arms had been yanked behind his back by Gage.

Reed bunched up the bouncer's collar, digging his fingers into the flesh at the base of the man's neck. He still couldn't believe Jeff was the culprit. His supposed *friend*, the man he'd done a solid for by giving him this job. That error of judgment, combined with the fact that Jeff had laid a hand on Darcy, was enough to make him go postal.

"You better hope the cops lock you up tonight," Reed hissed out. "Because if I find out you're not behind bars, I'm going to hunt you down and kill you."

AJ's calm voice penetrated the red haze of fury. "Get Darcy out of here, bro. We'll take care of this."

The urge to beat the living crap out of their traitorous bouncer was so powerful Reed could taste it on his lips, but he forced himself to release the man. Sucking in a breath, he whirled around and took Darcy's arm just as she staggered to her feet. Then he squared his jaw and dragged her out of the tiny space. He saw her mouth move, but couldn't hear what she said over the loud music or the deafening hammering of his heart.

Reed shoved open the emergency exit door and pulled her through it. As they entered the fluorescent-lit corridor, the music became muffled again, and Darcy's protests became audible.

"Where are we going? We should wait until the cops come!"

"You're not staying in this club a second longer," he snapped. He couldn't even look at her, afraid that if he saw the damage Jeff had done to her face, he might storm back inside and strangle the man with his bare hands. "You're leaving."

He tried to forcibly make her walk, but she didn't budge. "Reed, stop."

"Goddammit, am I going to have to carry you out of here myself?" When another objection left her lips, he scooped her off her feet. "I guess so."

Darcy's astonished squeak barely even registered. He flung her over his shoulder and marched toward the metal door at the hallway's end, ignoring her angry yelps and the small fists battering his back.

"Put me down right this instant! Oh my God, I can't believe you're doing this! I hate you so much right now!"

He didn't respond, didn't even acknowledge the squirming woman in his arms. To her credit, though, she was implementing a damn good worm, wiggling like a pro as she attempted to escape his grasp.

Only when they emerged into the alley that separated the club from the restaurant next door did he put her down.

Ignoring the death glare she shot him, he spoke in a low, deadly voice. "I have one question for you. And you better answer it right."

Aggravation darkened her eyes. "I can't believe you just carried me out of there like I was a five-year-old!"

"Answer the question, Darcy."

"You didn't ask one!"

He drew a calming breath. "What the hell were you thinking attacking Jeff like that?"

She looked amazed that he would even ask. "He had you pinned against the wall! I didn't want him to hurt you. I was trying to protect—"

"Wrong answer," he cut in. "The correct answer was, *I'm sorry, Reed. I was being stupid.*"

Her jaw fell open. "It was stupid of me to want to *help* you?"

"It was stupid of you to throw yourself at a man who's twice your size! He could have killed you!"

Reed's breathing was labored as he examined her face, running his shaky fingers over the red mark on her cheek. Jeff had hit her right on the cheekbone, and when Reed noticed the slight swelling there, red-hot anger bubbled in his stomach. The thought of Darcy getting hurt, and on his watch, made him want to smash his fist into the brick wall behind her head.

Afraid he'd say something he might regret, he gave her cheek one last caress before taking her hand and leading her toward the alley's entrance. He expected more protesting, but Darcy followed him silently, all the way to the main street and then around the side of the club to the parking lot behind it.

"My car's over there," she said in a tight voice.

Her displeased tone didn't spark even an iota of guilt or remorse. The shock of learning that Jeff was the one dealing drugs at Sin was nothing compared to the horror of seeing the man's elbow connect with Darcy's face. Protective urges he'd never known he possessed had reared their head, and they were surging through his blood now, refusing to let Darcy out of his sight.

He walked her to her older model hatchback, then gestured to her purse. "Keys," he said flatly.

She pulled her key ring out of her purse and wordlessly handed it over. Reed clicked the button to unlock the doors, then hovered over her while she settled in the driver's seat.

"You're behaving like a total Neanderthal," she muttered as she reached for the door handle.

Stifling his frustration, he rounded the vehicle and slid into the passenger side before she could drive away. "I won't apologize for being worried about you. You saw the look in Jeff's eyes—he was like a cornered animal. He would've knocked you unconscious if it meant escaping."

After a beat, Darcy spoke grudgingly. "Fine, I can see why you're upset."

He waited, but when she didn't continue, irritation seized his chest. "I still haven't heard an apology for you throwing yourself in the middle of a dangerous situation."

"I was trying to help you!"

"At the expense of your own safety? For fuck's sake, I thought you had more sense than that."

Her blue eyes blazed. "I'm hating you again. This whole alpha macho thing is annoying."

"Tough shit. I don't care if you're annoyed. The next time you're in the same room as a huge bouncer who's out for blood, stay far away from him, do you hear me?"

The insufferable woman had the nerve to give him a haughty look.

"Damn it, Darce. What's it gonna take to make you recognize how reckless you were? Am I going to have to fuck some sense into you? Is that it?"

Rather than the angry retort he expected, she responded with a gleam of defiance in her eyes. "Maybe you should."

In the blink of an eye, the tension in the car transformed into a thick canopy of heat.

With a low growl, Reed leaned over the center console and captured her lips in a hard kiss. Then he pulled back slightly, hissing a warning against her mouth. "You're trouble. Go home and put some ice on your cheek."

"No." She smirked at him.

"Darcy…"

"I don't feel like going home yet. So whatcha gonna do about it? Punish me?"

Sweet baby Jesus. No woman had *ever* aggravated him this much. And for someone who worked in an environment that revolved around enforcing rules and following directions, Darcy sure as hell didn't subscribe to her own teaching philosophy.

All she ever did was argue with him, challenge him, and at the moment, he was torn between yelling at her again, and ripping her clothes off and screwing her into silence.

Reed slowly released a breath. "Get in the backseat. Now."

It was almost comical how fast she scrambled. Her excitement incinerated the air, and he was surprised that the windows didn't fog up from all the heat she was radiating. But he didn't expect them to stay transparent for long. The temperature spiked by about a hundred degrees as he climbed into the back with her. It was hard to maneuver in such a cramped space, but luckily they didn't require much room for what he had in mind.

Slow and methodical, Reed undid the top button of her

jeans, his gaze glued to her flushed face. Her lips had parted, the anticipation in her eyes so powerful it seared right through him and turned his cock to granite.

"Next time I say *wait here*, you'd better goddamn listen." His voice was tinged with danger.

"Yeah, and what if I don't want to listen?" Darcy shot back.

He pushed her jeans down her hips, then freed one silky leg from the denim. Her black bikini panties were so skimpy they barely covered her mound, and his mouth filled with saliva as he stared at her creamy thighs.

"Then that would make you a bad girl, wouldn't it? And do you want to know what I do to bad girls?" Reed dragged his own zipper down, the tick-tick-tick of metallic teeth being released echoing in the car. "I fuck them. I fuck them hard."

"Oh God." Darcy squirmed beneath him, her arousal surrounding him like a seductive mist.

He cupped her damp panties with one hand and discovered that she was soaking wet. His cock pulsed, a jolt of need drawing his balls up tight. Christ almighty. He needed to be inside her more than he needed his next breath.

He eased his pants lower and released his cock from his boxer briefs. He paused to slip a condom packet out of his pocket, tore it open with his teeth, and sheathed himself. A second later, he drove his aching cock into her tight channel, so deep that the force of his hips had their bodies sliding toward the door and Darcy's head bumping the handle.

She didn't seem to care—her arms came around him, grasping the back of his head to bring him down for a kiss. Their mouths locked as he pumped inside her, over and over again, each unforgiving thrust stealing another piece of his sanity, another shard of his self-control.

"I couldn't handle it if something happened to you," he choked out, startled by the desperate note he heard in his voice.

Her eyes widened, lips parting in surprise. "Oh." She visibly swallowed as their bodies went still. "I'm fine, Reed. I really am. You don't have to worry about—"

He kissed her before she could finish, the adrenaline from the fight and the panic from seeing Darcy get hurt still burning like jet fuel in his bloodstream. Christ, he didn't want to think about any of that right now. He just wanted...needed...*her*.

Groaning, he resumed the frantic pace, determined to send both of them over the edge.

"Don't stop. Don't ever, ever stop." Her agonized pleas tickled his lips, and when she shifted her head and sank her teeth into his shoulder, Reed growled in pain and thrust harder.

He filled her with his cock, squeezing her breasts over her shirt as adrenaline and anger and concern and lust mingled together to fuel a furious tempo that set off a bone-melting release that spread through his body like waves of lava. He couldn't control it, couldn't wait for Darcy to reach that same earth-shattering apex, but fortunately she wasn't far behind, and his dick remained rock hard as he fucked her through her climax despite the fact that his own had turned his brain and body to jelly.

Darcy rocked beneath him, her body trembling as she rode out the orgasm. Her hot sheath squeezed him so tight his cock jerked inside her again, pulsing with pure, unadulterated ecstasy.

Groaning, Reed collapsed on top of her, doing his best not to crush her with his weight. Again, she didn't seem to mind, holding him close as she ran her fingers through his hair.

"I think I need to piss you off more often." The words shuddered out on a laugh. "Because I'm totally digging your choice of punishment."

Now that he'd come down from the orgasmic high and

his brain had started functioning again, the feeling of deep betrayal returned.

"I was the one who hired him," Reed mumbled. "Of all the stupid, irresponsible decisions—"

"Hey," she said firmly. "You didn't know what he was up to. You were just helping out a friend."

A friend. Ha. More like a fellow troublemaker from his fuck-up days.

Damn it, he should've known better than to trust Jeff. To believe that his old buddy had actually changed. Instead, he'd given the guy a goddamn *job*, and that mistake could have cost him and his friends their business.

"Seriously, Reed, you can't blame yourself for this. It's not your fault that he—"

The wail of sirens cut her off.

Sirens that didn't sound far away at all, but like they were coming from nearby.

Or, more accurately, from that very parking lot.

Reed froze as the red-and-blue lights shone through the windshield of their car, casting a ghostly glow over Darcy's face. He discreetly lifted his head, then swore when he spotted the two police cars cruising through the lot.

Shit. The cops had arrived to arrest Jeff.

Which would've been a fantastic thing—if Reed currently wasn't in the backseat of a car with his bare ass hanging out and his cock still lodged inside Darcy.

"Crap," he mumbled. "Don't make a single sound, Darce."

Obedience was too much to hope for.

Darcy took one look at the flashing lights, opened her mouth, and howled with laughter.

"Oh my God," she sputtered between giggles. "I can't believe this is happening."

Reed was forced to clamp his hand over her mouth to keep her quiet.

He doubted the officers could hear them, but damn it, he had no desire to get arrested for lewd conduct. On the one occasion he'd had the misfortune of landing in lockup—after a citation for public intoxication he and some fighting buddies were slapped with back when he was twenty—Reed had vowed to become a model citizen. Jail cells were too damn claustrophobic, and he'd be damned if he'd ever feel trapped like that again.

A minute ticked by, then another, until finally the lights on the police cruisers shut off. Footsteps thudded from the far end of the lot, near the club's back door. Male voices, more footsteps, doors slamming, and then the night was quiet again.

Reed carefully held the condom in place as he withdrew from Darcy's tight sheath. "I think the coast is clear."

Humor continued to dance in her eyes. "Am I a total weirdo for kind of wishing they'd caught us?"

"Yes." His response was swift and unequivocal.

"We would've gotten off with a warning," she protested. "Think of what a great story it could've made. All my friends have these awesome stories to tell, but nothing exciting *ever* happens to me."

This sure as hell qualified as exciting. He had to give her that.

Reed tucked the condom and torn package in his pocket, wincing as he pictured the mess it would make.

"I'm sure we can find some equally exciting things to do that don't result in us being arrested," he said ruefully.

She heaved out a dramatic sigh. "Fine. But I'm holding you to that."

Darcy wiggled into her pants and climbed back in the front seat, while Reed exited the car through the back door and then walked over to her window. She started the engine before rolling down the window, flashing him a beautiful smile that made his heart skip a beat. "See you tomorrow night?"

"Tomorrow morning," he corrected. "I'll stop by around nine to look at your cheek."

Darcy grumbled. "My cheek is just fine. I doubt there'll even be a bruise. You really don't have to—"

"I'll see you tomorrow morning." He leaned in to brush his lips over hers in a brief kiss, then marched off before she could argue again.

Chapter Twelve

Darcy opened the front door the next morning and found Reed standing behind it, one hand poised to knock.

"Hey," she squeaked, startled to see him. "What are you doing here?"

His expression was half amused, half smug. "I told you I'd come by to check on you." He glanced at his watch. "Huh, nine o'clock on the dot. I'm not usually so punctual."

She stifled a sigh. "I didn't think you were serious. And you didn't even call beforehand."

"Of course I didn't. Because we had prearranged plans." He flashed an arrogant look, then stepped forward and cupped her face with his hands.

She decided to humor him, allowing him to gently sweep his thumb over her skin as he examined her cheek. That crazy bouncer's elbow hadn't even left a mark, just like she'd known it wouldn't. But the way Reed's eyes clouded over, you'd think she'd been sporting a huge purple bruise.

"Does it hurt?"

"Not in the slightest," she answered cheerfully. "Hence

the complete lack of bruising, Reedford."

"Don't hence me," he chided. "I'm not the one who took a hit to the face last night."

"You *did* take a hit to the face! And you almost got strangled to death. I'm the one who should be putting my hands all over *you* to make sure *you're* okay."

He let his arms dangle at his sides, his expression epitomizing innocence. "Oh, I have no complaints about that. Please, put your hands all over me."

Jeez, the man was incorrigible. Darcy wondered if he purposely transmitted all that sexual energy, or if it just happened naturally. Either way, the end result remained the same—every time she saw him, she wanted to jump his bones.

When she didn't take the bait, Reed gestured to the empty canvas bags tucked over her purse. "Where are you headed?"

"The farmers market. I'm in desperate need of some fruits and veggies, and I don't like to get them at the grocery store. They're never as fresh or as tasty." She shifted her purse to her other shoulder so she could lock the apartment door. "Oh, and one of the vendors there sells the best homemade jams and jellies. I swear, they're to die for. Especially the strawberry jam."

"You had me at strawberry jam."

"That was the last thing I said!"

"Was it?" His tone was breezy. "Anyway, should we take my car or yours?"

Darcy blinked. "What are you talking about?"

"How would you like to get to the market?" He spoke slowly, as if she were a non-English-speaking immigrant who'd just stepped onto American soil. "In my vehicle or yours?"

He wanted to come with her?

Reluctance seized her chest. No, he definitely couldn't do that. She'd *specifically* told him that she only wanted sex. So unless they showed up at the market naked and fucked on a pile of tomatoes, letting him come along compromised her entire stance. Farmers markets were notoriously known for being relationship places. If she and Reed visited one together, they'd be taking the first step toward coupledom.

Which meant she had to put her foot down and lay down the law again.

Except she'd underestimated his tenacity.

"My car," he decided. "It's faster than yours. We don't want to get there too late and find out that all the jam is sold out. Here, want me to carry your bags?" Without letting her answer, he swiped the empty sacks and tucked them under his arm, then took off walking.

Darcy gaped at his retreating back. And then her gaze lowered to his perfect ass, hugged by faded blue jeans, and for a moment there she forgot where she was. All she could think about was how good it felt to squeeze those firm buttocks when Reed was plunging his cock inside her.

It took a second to snap out of her dirty trance, and by then, Reed was already at the elevator, tossing her an expectant look over his shoulder.

Well. Clearly the man wasn't taking no for an answer, so why not let him tag along? Besides, she planned on buying a ton of stuff, so she might as well put all those glorious muscles of his to good use and force him to carry her bags.

"So what happened to Jeff?" she asked as they stepped into the elevator.

Reed instantly tensed. "He was arrested after you left."

"Good. Another dealer off the streets, right?"

The dark cloud on his face didn't dissipate. "Yup. And now I get to spend the rest of my life apologizing to Gage and AJ for bringing that scumbag into the club."

"Reed, it's not your—"

"Fault," he finished, his bitter expression a clear indication that he didn't want to pursue the subject any longer.

Darcy didn't push him, going quiet as they rode the elevator to the lobby and headed outside where Reed's black Camaro waited at the curb. She slid into the passenger seat, breathing in the clean pine fragrance intermixed with the spicy masculine scent she was growing accustomed to. Or addicted to. Either one worked.

Reed started the car and merged into traffic. He drove toward the stop sign at the end of the street, stopped dutifully, then took a left turn and said, "We're going to Haymarket, right? Or did you want to hit Copley Square?"

Darcy had to scrape her jaw off the car floor. "Haymarket. And how are you so knowledgeable about the city's farmers markets?"

He shrugged, his foot easing up on the gas as they neared a red light. "My uncle used to date this woman who made her own cheese. She sold her stuff at a different market every weekend, all over the East Coast, and Uncle Colin always forced me to go with him."

A hundred more questions bit at Darcy's tongue. She suddenly realized she didn't know a thing about Reed's background. Who his parents were, where he'd gone to school, why he'd chosen to fight professionally.

She swallowed her curiosity, clinging to the swift reminder that she wasn't allowed to get to know him outside the carnal sense. That would only land her in hot water. She would get attached like she always did, and then all her hopes for a harmless, no-heartbreak fling would go up in flames.

Still, her silence brought a rush of guilt. Darcy had never felt ruder in her life as she fixed her gaze out the window and pretended to admire the scenery she'd seen thousands of times before. The lack of interaction bothered her, but not as much as the one-word responses she offered when Reed tried to engage her in conversation.

For a woman whose middle name was *chatty*, keeping

a conversational distance was excruciating. Reed didn't comment on her sudden change of personality, but he did shoot several contemplative glances her way throughout the entire drive.

Twenty minutes later, they entered the enormous outdoor market and joined the crowd of people already filling the large space. It was mid-September, and the temperature was still in the high eighties, much to Darcy's pleasure. She was hoping the good weather followed them all the way to October, the month she'd drawn for her recess chaperoning duties at school. But she already knew her October stint would be a gazillion times better than last year, when she'd shivered in the playground for the entire month of February during one of the worst winters to ever hit Boston.

"Where should we go first?" Reed asked.

Darcy's gaze roamed the rows and rows of tables that made up the market. "Let's start with veggies, then hit the fruit stands, and finish up with some jam tasting."

"Sounds like a plan."

With his fingers loosely hooked on his belt loops, he walked alongside her toward the tables of vegetables to their right. For the next half hour, they embarked on a health-conscious shopping spree, Reed carrying their overflowing bags without Darcy even having to ask. The whole time, he chatted easily about nothing in particular, while she did her damnedest to avoid any deep conversation. Despite the fact that she'd choked down so many potential questions her throat had run dry from the constant gulping, she was proud of herself for resisting temptation.

But the dark side finally called her over. They'd just stopped at a table piled high with Red Delicious apples when Reed broke out in laughter.

"Shit. I still can't look at apples without thinking about this girl I knew in middle school."

Darcy had to grin. "Why, was her name *Apple*?"

"Actually, it was," he said smugly. "Apple Schulman, the product of a hippie mom and Jewish dad. She was skinny as a rail with big brown eyes and a mouthful of braces, and I was utterly and completely in love with her."

"How old were you?"

"Twelve, I think? It was the sixth grade. She sat in front of me for every class, and I'd spend hours daydreaming about her and trying to work up the courage to ask her out. All the grades had their own annual dances, and I'd already chickened out about inviting her to the sixth grade one, but there was also this big school-wide dance at the end of the year." Reed chuckled. "I was dying for Apple to go with me, but I was too terrified to ask. Every time I walked up to her locker, I'd freeze up like a Popsicle and then scurry away."

Darcy laughed. She had trouble picturing the scene he was describing. The Reed she knew oozed confidence and sex appeal. She couldn't imagine him ever being too nervous to talk to someone, or that any girl, old or young, would ever turn down an offer to date him.

You did.

She banished the internal accusation. That was different. She was a grown woman, not a sixth grader who'd shriek in delight if she scored a date to the school dance. Darcy was smart enough to know what she wanted from her future. And sure, Reed was great in bed, but she wasn't entirely convinced he could be what she needed *out* of it—dependable, compassionate, cautious rather than impulsive.

Some women liked a man who was reckless. God knew Darcy had liked it last night when Reed ravished her in the backseat of her car after throwing the equivalent of a temper tantrum. But just because he excited her didn't mean he could satisfy her emotionally.

"Anyway, in the end," Reed continued, "after I realized

talking to Apple wasn't a viable option, I decided to give her a note."

"What did it say?" Darcy asked curiously.

He snickered. "It said *do you love me?* And underneath the question were two boxes, one for *yes* and one for *no*. I told her to check the box that best described her feelings."

Darcy burst out laughing. "Dude, that's pretty bold for a sixth-grade boy."

"That's how I roll, baby. Bold and ballsy to the bitter end."

Her tone softened. "Awwww. *Was* it a bitter end? Did she check the *no* box?"

"Nope." Reed grinned. "She added a new box that said *maybe*. And below that she wrote *I'll tell you after you take me to the dance.*"

"Go you," Darcy said, clapping her hands in teasing applause. "So you got the girl."

"Sure did." He released a glum breath. "At least until the dance. Halfway through the second Mariah Carey ballad, this kid named Scotty Dawson cut in and whisked Apple away, and they were boyfriend and girlfriend by the time her parents came to pick us up. As you can probably guess, that was one awkward car ride home."

"Oh, that's so awful. I can't believe she did that." Darcy glowered in defense of the twelve-year-old Reed. "What a bi-otch."

"Naah, she wasn't a bi-otch. Just a fickle sixth-grade girl. I actually have her on my Facebook."

Darcy snorted. "Really?"

"Yup, but she's Apple Shulman-Schwartz now. Married a nice Jewish boy, popped out five kids, and works as an estate lawyer at a fancy-pants firm in Beacon Hill."

"Impressive."

"I know, right? And then there's me," he said wryly. "A total bum, not even paying a mortgage because I'm living in the house I inherited from my uncle. And running a night club, which, by the way, is a job Apple would probably consider scandalous."

Darcy snapped to his defense again. "Hey, you've got nothing to be ashamed of. First of all, you're a business owner, which is just as impressive as being a lawyer, and who cares if you inherited your house instead of buying it? You're still responsible for all your household bills, and insurance, and all that important stuff. You're smart, and responsible, and—" She halted, feeling like scolding herself for letting the conversation take such a dangerous turn.

She was supposed to be making an effort *not* to see him as any of those things. Reed was the bad boy hottie she was sleeping with, the man who was giving her a crash course in passion before she moved on and reverted back to her relationship ways.

"And sexy," she finished, hastily veering back to safe territory. "Like, ridiculously sexy. Did I tell you how hot you look today?"

"Nope, you didn't. But I sure would love to hear it." He waggled his eyebrows suggestively.

"Okay, well, that shirt? Just tight enough to outline all those yummy muscles. And the way your butt fills out those jeans? Hubba hubba."

Reed threw his head back and laughed. "Gee, I had no idea I was talking to Bazooka Joe."

"I'm serious, you look so good in those jeans I want to rip them off you." Darcy glanced past his impossibly broad shoulders, catching sight of something that made her raise one brow in challenge. "In fact, why don't we duck in there so I can do just that?"

He twisted around, chuckling when he spotted the rickety little shed a dozen yards from where they stood. It was tucked behind a row of empty tables, its wooden door gaping open to reveal the stacks of crates inside of it.

"Are you seriously suggesting we get it on in the middle of the farmers market?" Reed drawled.

Darcy had been half joking, but the second he said the words, her thighs clenched so hard she nearly pulled a muscle.

She slowly met Reed's gaze. "No, I'm suggesting we get it on in a *shed* in the middle of the farmers market."

Unmistakable interest lit his vivid blue eyes.

"Well?" she prompted.

"Lead the way, baby." He answered with no hesitation, and a whole lot of mischief.

Her pulse sped up as she laced her fingers through his and tugged him toward the shed. Reed laughed in surprise, but she noticed that not a single protest left his mouth as the two of them ever so casually approached the small structure. Darcy furtively glanced around to make sure nobody was looking, then pulled Reed inside and closed the door.

Darkness instantly enveloped them, but several sliver-thin gaps in the wooden door allowed for shards of light to slice into the cramped space. She glimpsed dust motes dancing over Reed's head, and wrinkled her nose at the odor of dirt, oil and sawdust. But at least it didn't smell like rotting fruits and vegetables, so that was a plus.

There was also no lock, but luckily the door did latch, and Darcy knew it would stay latched, because Reed leaned his back against it as he jerked her toward him.

His mouth met hers, and the urgency of his kiss robbed her of breath. His lips devoured hers, his slick tongue entering her mouth in one sensual glide. He cupped her ass and brought her lower body flush to his, rotating his hips so she could feel every tantalizing inch of his arousal. Heart pounding, Darcy rubbed up against him like an attention-starved cat, moaning when his mouth dropped to her neck to kiss her feverish flesh.

Her hands fumbled for the button of her jeans, and she

cursed herself for not wearing a skirt. She really, really needed to start wearing more skirts.

And the notion that she was now basing her fashion decisions on how easily she could grant Reed Miller access to her body didn't even bother her. She wanted him inside her, *now*, and damn her stupid pants for getting in the way.

When Reed released a groan of dismay, she realized that her clothing situation was the least of their concerns. "I don't have a condom," he told her.

She groaned too. "Neither do I. We used up the stash in my purse when you came over yesterday after school." She wasn't on the pill because it gave her terrible migraines, and no way was she risking having sex without birth control.

But she'd also be damned if they went back outside without at least one of them orgasming first.

"You're not leaving this shed until you come," she declared. "Undo your pants so I can suck you off."

He responded with a smirk. "Undo yours so I can finger you."

They stared at each other in a sexual standoff, until Reed gave her an innocent look and said, "If I finger you first, I'll be able to lick your juices off my hand, and trust me, I'll come so fast if I'm tasting you on my lips when you're blowing me."

A strangled moan flew out. Darcy hurriedly unzipped her jeans, and a second later Reed's warm hand slid inside her panties, his skillful fingers seeking out her clit. He rubbed the sensitive nub with his index finger, steady, circular motions that made her tingle.

She was awed by the look of sheer concentration on his face, the steely determination, as if his entire purpose in life was to make her come.

She was too sexed up, too primed, too excited by the fact that they were doing this in a paper-thin structure in the middle of her favorite farmers market. The muffled voices and carefree laughter coming from behind the door only fueled that excitement, and when Reed pushed two fingers inside her she had to bite her lip to stop from crying out.

"Oh baby, this gets you so hot, doesn't it? Getting fingered while all those people walk around outside that door, totally oblivious." His voice was raspy. Mocking. Seductive. "What would they think if they knew what I was doing to you right now? What would they do if they saw you biting your lip like that, if they felt how wet you are? My fingers are soaked, baby."

With a sinful smile, he curled his hand and stroked her G spot, and Darcy exploded in a hot rush. She cut off her own scream by burying her face in Reed's chest and using his shirt as a gag. She felt his heart pounding against her cheek and realized he was as excited as she was. That getting her off just now had affected him as much as it had her.

The moment she was coherent enough to function, Darcy dropped to her knees and had his cock out of his pants in record speed. Now it was Reed who was biting his lip to keep from making noise. Reed who was trembling from her touch.

His features stretched tight as she wrapped her lips around the head of his cock and sucked.

"Hell in a hand basket," he burst out. "I'm gonna come."

Her muffled laughter echoed in the darkness, and she nearly choked on his cock thanks to the giggles that overtook her.

Darcy had never known true feminine power until this very moment. One teasing suck and she'd utterly destroyed him, turned him into a grunting, shuddering mess as he came inside her mouth. If they were having sex, maybe she wouldn't have been so pleased with the one-thrust show, but right now, she welcomed the hot pulses that coated her tongue, eagerly drinking in the salty, masculine taste of him. She tightened her suction on his cock so she could suck him dry, swallowing every last drop of his pleasure.

"Christ. Fuck, Darcy. You don't know how good that feels."

He groaned softly as he withdrew from her mouth, then hauled her up and kissed her so deeply she swayed on her feet.

When they pulled apart, they were both grinning like idiots.

"That was...fun," she remarked.

His muffled laughter tickled her forehead. "Uh-huh. Fun."

She quickly zipped up her pants, then his, because he seemed too dazed to do it himself. But evidently she hadn't robbed him of *all* his faculties, because when she reached for the door latch, he intercepted her hand with a knowing look.

"I know what you're doing," he said mockingly.

She furrowed her brow. "Huh?"

"You've been doing it all morning. You're trying to keep me at a distance. Avoiding important topics, distracting me with sex when the conversation gets too serious for your liking."

Darcy's cheeks grew warm as he called her out on it. Reed had never come off as very perceptive, so either she'd been wrong about that, or she was way more transparent than she'd thought.

Either way, she felt like a total ass. "I'm sorry," she said softly. "You're right, that's what I've been doing. It's just...I meant what I said when we started this. I don't want anything more than a fling."

"Don't worry, Darce. It's still a fling." The hint of a smile crossed his face. "For now."

Then he opened the door and strode out of the shed, leaving her staring after him in dismay.

For now? Crap. What did he mean by that? What the heck was that stubborn man up to?

And why did she get the most unsettling feeling she wasn't going to like it?

Or...an even scarier thought...that maybe she'd like it *too much*.

Chapter Thirteen

"Did you see that?" Devon was grinning from ear to ear as he turned to check if Reed had witnessed the perfect spiral the kid had just thrown.

Granted, the football hadn't sailed more than fifteen feet in the air—and landed nowhere close to the target they'd set up—but Reed wasn't about to point that out. Or complain. Because damn, the kid really *had* mastered the art of the spiral. And after only two tries, no less.

"That was awesome," he called out. "A few more throws and you'll be giving Tom Brady a run for his money."

The eleven-year-old boy bounded across the grassy field toward Reed, sidling up to him as he went to retrieve the football. This was their second official "outing," after Darcy's school had gotten in contact with Reed two weeks ago.

Apparently Devon hadn't stopped raving to his mother about Reed's defense workshop, so much so that Monique Pearson had asked the school for Reed's number and called him up out of the blue.

Devon's mother had revealed she'd recently enrolled

her son in the Big Brother program, but that he'd yet to find anyone he really connected with. When she'd asked Reed if he would consider joining the program and being paired up with Devon, he hadn't had the heart to say no.

And now he was glad he'd agreed. He absolutely adored the kid and found himself looking forward to these Sunday afternoon outings. Their allotted two hours had flown by today, and Devon looked disappointed as they left the football field behind the high school and walked to the parking lot.

"Are you sure you can't come for dinner?" Devon asked, his bottom lip sticking out.

Reed shook his head regretfully. "Sorry, kiddo, I really can't. I start work at seven, and I have a few things to take care of before that."

Devon sighed loudly. "*Fine*."

He ruffled the kid's curly hair and smiled. "How about next week? If it's okay with your mom, maybe I'll stop by for an early dinner before work."

The boy's face lit up. "Yes! I'll ask her the second we get home!"

Chuckling at the kid's enthusiasm, Reed unlocked the car and opened the passenger door for Devon. Once they'd both settled in and buckled up, he drove in the direction of Devon's apartment building in Dorchester.

Ten minutes later, Reed walked the boy up to his fifth floor apartment, greeting Devon's mother with a smile after she'd opened the door.

"Did you boys have fun?" Monique asked.

As usual, the woman looked incredibly frazzled. Reed had learned that she worked two jobs—full-time hours during the week for the first one, and a weekend graveyard shift for the second, which meant that Devon's grandmother stayed with them when Monique worked the overnighters. Reed didn't envy the woman, but he sure as hell respected her work ethic, not to mention her determination to provide a good life for her son.

"Reed is gonna come over for dinner next weekend!" Devon told his mother. "Is that okay?"

An indulgent smile lifted her lips. Reed got the feeling that she rarely said no to her son, not if she could help it.

"Sounds good to me." Her grateful gaze shifted to Reed. "Thank you. You've been wonderful with him."

His cheeks warmed up from the praise. "My pleasure. He's a great kid." Reed ruffled Devon's hair again. "I'll see you next Sunday, kiddo."

There was a spring to his step as he left the building. Man, he truly loved spending time with that kid.

And he also loved spending time with Darcy, which he was also about to do.

It had been two weeks since their illicit visit to the farmers market, and in those two weeks, Reed had steadily been making headway with her. All those pesky rules she'd initially tried to enforce were crumbling away one by one.

No sleepovers? They crashed at each other's places all the time.

No dinners? They'd gone for Italian just the other night.

No heavy conversation? Last week they'd stayed up all night talking about their families.

Oh yeah, he was definitely wearing her down.

Even though Darcy still insisted it was a fling, he knew damn well that it wasn't. At least not for him. He loved every second he spent with her, and not just the sex part. He loved sending her those cheesy text messages that he knew made her smile. He loved her silly jokes. Her laughter. Snuggling in bed together after they'd rocked each other's worlds.

Christ, he liked her so damn much.

No, it was more than like. He was falling for her, and he was helpless to stop it.

He *didn't* want to stop it.

And he was confident that sooner or later Darcy would admit she was falling for him, too. She *had* to. He was trying so damn hard to show her that she could count on him, but he'd also promised himself not to push her—he wanted her to reach that conclusion all by herself.

Reed had two hours before he needed to head over to Sin, which gave him and Darcy plenty of time to get into all sorts of wicked trouble, but when he knocked on her door twenty minutes later, his anticipation was instantly snuffed out.

"Oh, crap," she blurted when she saw him. "Didn't you get my message? I can't hang out today."

He furrowed his brow, then reached into his pocket for his phone. When a black screen greeted him, he cursed under his breath. "It's dead. I guess I forgot to charge it this morning." Reed studied her flustered expression. "What's going on?"

Darcy raked a hand through her hair. She'd worn it loose and it fell over one shoulder, the wavy strands hovering over the V neckline of her white T-shirt. Her dark-blue skinny jeans hugged her shapely legs, and when Reed glanced at her feet, her yellow flip-flops and bright red toenails made him smile. She was so fucking pretty his heart squeezed.

"My dad's in town." Her flat tone revealed her precise thoughts on the matter.

During one of their many no-longer-forbidden conversations, Darcy had told him all about her father and how he swept into town a few times a year before disappearing again for months. In Reed's opinion, the man sounded like a total jackass. A selfish jerk who'd run out on his wife and daughter.

But he hadn't voiced his opinion to Darcy. No matter how unreliable her old man was, he was still her old man.

"Did you know he was coming?" Reed asked.

She shook her head, her jaw tighter than a drum. "Of

course not. I *never* know when he's coming." A buzzing drew her gaze to the phone in her hand. She looked at the screen, then groaned in annoyance. "God, this is insane. He says he wants to see me, but he keeps changing the plans. We were supposed to have lunch at the harbor, but now he wants to meet at the Starbucks around the corner from here."

"I guess I'll head out then." Reed leaned in to brush a kiss over her lips. He was tempted to turn it into a hot make-out session, but he knew now wasn't the time.

When he pulled back, he found Darcy eyeing him miserably. "What's wrong?" he asked.

Her next words startled him. "Do you… Will you come with me?"

Reed tried not to gape at her. She was inviting him to meet her father?

Granted, that hadn't been one of the items on her *no* list, but that was probably because it hadn't even occurred to her that it could happen.

"I just think…" She shrugged. "Maybe if I bring someone along it won't be as awkward as it usually is."

Or it would be a hundred times *more* awkward, Reed almost pointed out.

When he hesitated, Darcy's blue eyes grew resigned. "Sorry, forget it. I guess it's a stupid idea—"

"Sure," he interrupted. "I'll come."

"You will?"

Reed nodded.

The next thing he knew, Darcy threw her arms around him, stood up on her tiptoes, and kissed him. No tongue, but he tasted the overpowering relief on her lips as their mouths met. His heart clenched again, a wave of emotion floating through him. He was entirely touched that she trusted him enough to introduce him to her dad, to expose him to what he knew was a painful relationship in her life.

Reed stroked her cheek with his thumb, then smiled. "When do we have to go?"

"Now," she said glumly.

His index finger teased her bottom lip. "Aw, quit being a brat. I'm sure it won't be as bad as you think."

"Yeah, maybe you're right."

But Reed was wrong.

It ended up being even *worse*.

The moment they strode into the coffee shop, he felt like a tornado had swept through the room. Stuart Grant's presence was *that* ferocious.

"Darcy! Honey!" A tall, burly man with dirty-blond hair and sparkling blue eyes flew out of his chair at a table in the back and dashed across the room to pull Darcy into a huge bear hug.

"Hey, Dad." She laughed as he lifted her off her feet, then leaned in to give him a quick kiss on the cheek. Her father had the leathery skin of a man who spent a lot of time in the sun, though Reed wasn't sure how that was possible considering Stuart sat in the cab of a truck ten hours a day.

"This is my friend Reed," she introduced.

Friend?

Oh *hell* no.

Before Reed could correct her, Stuart distracted him with a dazzling smile that could have lit up Times Square. The laugh lines around the older man's mouth told Reed that smiles were readily available when it came to Darcy's dad, but Reed couldn't help but feel there was something very superficial about that gleaming, white-toothed grin.

"So nice to meet you!" Stuart heartily pumped Reed's hand before clapping him on the shoulder.

He was taken aback by the overwhelming enthusiasm. "Uh, nice to meet you too."

Darcy gestured to the counter. "Why don't we order some

coffees and then—"

"Oh, I can't stay," her father interrupted.

She blinked. "What?"

"I need to get back on the road. I thought I'd have more time, but the shipment's delivery date was pushed up. I just wanted to see my best girl and give her a hug before I took off."

Reed swallowed his disbelief. Was this a fucking joke? What kind of father couldn't spare even five minutes for his only kid?

What kind of father couldn't sit down and have one measly coffee with the daughter he hadn't seen in six months?

"Are you doing okay for money?" Stuart asked cheerfully, oblivious to the fact that Darcy was gawking at him as if he'd grown horns.

She blinked again, rapidly, as if trying to make sense of the nonsensical situation. "I, ah, I'm fine. I—"

"Here, take this just in case." In a blur of motion, her father whipped out his wallet and extracted several hundred-dollar bills, then tucked them in Darcy's limp hand.

She kept shaking her head, mumbled something incoherent, but her smiling, ignorant father just wrapped his arms around her in another big hug.

"I promise I'll have more time to spend with you on my next visit." Stuart grasped her chin, then smacked a loud kiss on her cheek. "You look beautiful. Teaching must agree with you."

"I..." Darcy blinked at least twenty more times.

"Okay, honey, time to head out." He aimed a brilliant smile at her, clapped Reed's shoulder again, and then he was gone, dashing out of the coffee house in another tornado of energy.

Reed stared at the door, unable to fathom what had just happened. He was tempted to run after him and beat him senseless for his sheer insensitivity, his utter obliviousness, but the soft noise that tore out of Darcy's throat rendered that course of action impossible.

When he shifted his head and saw her expression, his heart cracked in two. Tears clung to her thick eyelashes, her face was paler than the white wall behind her, and her hand had curled into a fist, crumpling the bills her father had shoved into it.

Since they were standing in the middle of Starbucks, nearly all the patrons were watching them curiously, and Reed's protective instincts swiftly kicked in. Not wanting a bunch of strangers to witness Darcy's tears, he wasted no time taking her hand and leading her out of the coffee shop.

The moment they stepped onto the sidewalk, Darcy's face collapsed and the tears streamed out.

"Oh, baby, c'mere." He pulled her into his arms and held her tight, stroking her hair as she shook against him.

Several pedestrians shot them curious looks, but Reed was too focused on Darcy to care. He ran his fingers through her hair in a soothing motion, wishing like hell that Stuart Grant were there so he could kick that bastard's ass.

"I don't know why I'm even surprised," she mumbled between sobs. "I don't know why I'm upset."

"Because he's your father, and he let you down," Reed said roughly.

She wrenched out of his embrace, anger burning in her eyes. "Ten fucking minutes. He couldn't spare *ten fucking minutes* for me?" Her incensed gaze dropped to the money she was still holding. "What kind of man does this?"

Pain and sympathy squeezed Reed's chest. "I'm so sorry, Darce. You deserve so much better than that."

"I do!" she burst out. "I *do* deserve better!" She furiously swiped at her cheeks with the sleeve of her thin cardigan. "I am *not* going to cry over that jerk. He doesn't *deserve* my tears."

When her arm came down and he saw her face, Reed's lips twitched.

"What?" she demanded. "Why are you smiling?"

He swallowed a chuckle. "Because..." The laugh slipped out. "You must've brushed up against some grease or something when we were walking over, because your face is covered with it."

Her cheeks turned bright red. "It is?"

He nodded.

"Is it bad?"

He nodded again.

"Crap."

Fighting to keep from laughing again, Reed licked the pads of two fingers and brought them to the black marks streaking across her face. As he quickly wiped them away, he noticed Darcy staring at him in awe.

"What?" he said thickly.

"You're a really good guy, Reed." Her voice wobbled. "Like, a *really* good guy."

He couldn't fight the rush of pleasure that flooded his chest. He'd been waiting for weeks to see that shift of emotion in her eyes, for her to realize that he was more than a good lay.

That he truly did have more to offer her.

"Yeah, I guess I'm not so bad," he said lightly.

Her expression softened as she reached for his hand. She laced her fingers through his. "No, I guess you're not."

Reed dipped his head and gave her a soft, fleeting kiss. "Come on," he said. "Let's go back to your place. Your afternoon schedule seems to have cleared up, which means it's officially become my job to make you forget everything that just happened."

Darcy smiled through her tears. "I'm holding you to that."

Chapter Fourteen

That Friday, Darcy didn't leave the school until two hours after the final bell. To her annoyance, the monthly staff meeting had run late, thanks to an argument between two teachers about whether Wikipedia was considered a legitimate citation source. Personally, she didn't give a shit as long as her students only used Wiki pages with multiple sources, but Marge, the history teacher had refused to let up, effectively putting a damper on everyone's TGIF.

"Holy cow, how much did you want to punch Marge in the face?" Shannon demanded as they crossed the empty parking lot.

"So frickin' bad," Darcy replied with a sigh.

"See, now if *I* said that?" Shannon's husband Tom piped up. "I'd probably get thrown in jail for even *talking* about hitting a woman." His brown eyes flickered with amusement. "But goddamn, someone needs to tell that broad that screaming like a banshee isn't the way to get what you want."

Darcy wholeheartedly agreed—her ears were still ringing from Marge's high-pitched shouts.

The trio reached Shannon and Tom's SUV, stopping so Darcy could exchange quick hugs with both her friends. "Are we still on for girls' night next week?" she asked Shannon.

"Absolutely." Shannon poked her husband in the arm. "It's the only time I get some peace and quiet."

Tom raised his eyebrows. "Says the woman who takes hour-long bubble baths every night. Where's *my* bath time, missy?"

"If you're nice, I'll let you join me in the tub tonight," his wife answered.

"Define nice."

"Hmmm. Well, cooking me dinner would qualify. And then doing the dishes. And then taking out the garbage. And then—"

"Forget it. I'll just catch a quick shower," Tom interrupted. "See you Monday, Darce."

He hopped into the driver's seat so fast Darcy couldn't help but giggle. "That man seriously hates chores, huh?"

"Tell me about it. But the threat of chores is the only way to get him to back off about the bath thing. It really is my favorite me-time activity." Shannon winked. "Did I tell you about that new waterproof vibrator I bought?"

Darcy rolled her eyes. "Yes. Many, many times. And no, I'm not interested in procuring my own. Big green Bob is all I need."

"Oh really? Are you sure you don't mean big not-green *Reed*?" Shannon wiggled her eyebrows. "Because your fling doesn't seem to be ending, hon."

Nope, it certainly, mind-bogglingly *wasn't*. Darcy still had no idea how it happened, but somehow the fling had reached the one-month mark. She'd expected it to fizzle out by now, and yet...it hadn't.

"So when are you going to admit you're in a relationship with the guy?" Shannon teased.

Alarm skittered up her spine. "I'm not. I mean, we're not. We're still just—"

A loud honk interrupted her incoherent stammering.

Darcy turned her head in time to see an unfamiliar white sedan speed into the lot. She peered at the windshield, then relaxed when she recognized the driver.

"That's Devon's mom. I should go over and say hello."

"Uh-huh. Wonderful diversion tactic," Shannon said with a smirk. "But don't think you're off the hook, hon. I plan on going over this topic in depth next Wednesday at girls' night."

Laughing, Darcy's co-worker hopped into the SUV, and then Shannon and Tom were gone, leaving her to stride over to Monique Pearson's car alone.

"Ms. Grant, it's so good to see you." The pretty African-American woman greeted her with a smile as she got out of the car. "I've been meaning to call you for weeks now, but work and Devon keep me so busy I keep forgetting."

She offered a warm smile in return. "I understand. Devon's waiting for you inside." She paused. "By the way, I wanted to ask you—do you have another son? I heard Devon talking with some of the other kids the other day about his older brother, and I was surprised because I didn't think he had one."

Monique chuckled. "Oh, he was referring to Reed."

Confusion washed over her. "Reed?"

"Yes. That's actually what I wanted to speak to you about. I wanted to thank you for setting up that self-defense workshop. Devon learned a lot, and he got a big brother out of it, too. I got in touch with Reed after Devon wouldn't stop gushing about how 'awesomesauce' he was." The woman used air quotes, her mouth twitching with humor. "When I mentioned to Reed that Devon was in the Big Brother program, he agreed to join up."

Darcy's bewilderment only grew. "He did?"

Monique nodded. "He takes Devon out every Sunday."

"He does?"

"The arrangement seems to be working well so far, and I really wanted to thank you for introducing them. My son absolutely adores Reed." The woman glanced at her watch. "Anyway, I need to grab Devon. Thanks again, Ms. Grant."

Darcy watched the other woman walk away, stunned by what she'd heard. Four Sundays had passed since the workshop, but Reed hadn't said a word to her about signing up to be Devon's big brother.

Why the omission, though? She'd quickly discovered this past month that Reed didn't shy away from any topic, and the two of them had had plenty of conversations about her students, so why hadn't he mentioned his arrangement with Devon?

The fact that he'd kept it from her was totally mystifying.

Frowning, Darcy headed to her car and unlocked the doors. She would definitely have to ask Reed about it tonight. He was coming over after he finished work, which meant she'd have to take a very long nap when she got home so she wouldn't be a zombie when he showed up at three in the morning. But she honestly wasn't complaining, since Reed always made sure to reward her for her staying-awake efforts.

It was actually kind of scary how the sex only seemed to get better, and she knew that had contributed to her complete lack of motivation to end the fling. She'd gone into it craving passion—well, the passion kept coming. And coming. And coming.

Maybe if the sex was bad, she could find the willpower to call things off, but each time Reed kissed her, or touched her, or fucked her to yet another mind-blowing orgasm, she seemed to forget that their arrangement was supposed to be temporary.

Sighing, Darcy drove out of the lot, her mind drifting back to the revelation that Reed was spending his Sundays with his "little brother." At least now it made sense why he always seemed to be busy when she suggested they do something on Sunday afternoons.

God, she had no idea how she felt about him anymore. Every time she tried to slap that bad boy label on him, he turned around and proved that he was anything but. Comforting her the day she'd been crushed by her father's disgusting display of selfishness. Pulling out her chair when they went out for dinner. Letting her squeeze his hand to the point of bone-breaking when they'd gone to see a horror movie last week.

Spending his free time with a little boy who needed a father figure.

Darcy bit down hard on her bottom lip as she stopped at a red light.

Crap. It was becoming glaringly obvious that she needed to reevaluate this fling of theirs. She was really starting to care about Reed, her initial doubts floating away like dandelions in the wind.

But at the same time, a part of her still feared this was just a lark on Reed's part. He'd said so himself—he'd never lasted more than a month when it came to relationships. Darcy was afraid his impulsive nature would suddenly rear its head, he'd get bored with her, and then he'd move on to the next exciting affair and leave her heartbroken.

And was that a risk she really wanted to take?

・・・

Reed was dead-ass tired when he got to Darcy's apartment that night. Or morning. Time lost all meaning when you worked at a nightclub.

The second he saw her beautiful face, though, he snapped

into a state of wide awake. As bad as he felt showing up so late, this was his favorite time to see her. When she was sleepy, hair tousled, wearing her pajamas.

Her body was warm and pliant as she sank into his embrace and greeted him with a happy sigh. "You got here just in time. The coffee's wearing off."

He chuckled.

"Seriously, I'm going to turn back into a pumpkin in about ten minutes. Kiss me now before it's too late."

Like he could ever turn down *that* offer.

Reed kissed her, hard and deep, until she was gasping against his mouth. When her tongue darted out to swirl over his, he groaned as the sweet flavor of her suffused his taste buds. He could never get his fill of this woman. Never.

"Wait." She broke off the kiss with a breathy exhale, her blue eyes hazy. "I have to ask you something before my brain totally turns to jelly."

Reed cocked a brow. "Ask away."

"Why didn't you tell me you signed up for the Big Brother program?"

The question caught him off guard, bringing a pang of discomfort to his chest. Darcy didn't look angry, but he knew from her perplexed face that she was bothered by it.

"I…ah…I don't know," he said gruffly. "I just didn't."

The half-ass response didn't satisfy her, just as he'd known it wouldn't. "You just didn't?" she echoed, sounding even more confused.

Reed edged toward the living room couch, where he sat and raked a hand through his hair. A moment later, Darcy flopped down beside him and settled in a cross-legged position.

"Stop being mysterious," she said. "I want to know why you kept it a secret."

"It wasn't a secret. I just didn't mention it."

She snorted. "That's still a secret in my book."

Reed released a sigh. "I guess at first it was because you made it clear you didn't want to talk about important stuff." He didn't miss the guilt that flashed in her eyes. "And then...I dunno...I didn't say anything because I didn't want you to think it was something I was doing for *you*. You know, to impress you, or try to make you like me more."

Her forehead creased. "Okay..."

He paused, trying to vocalize his messed up rationale. "It was something I was doing for *me*. I mean, I signed up because Monique Pearson pretty much twisted my arm into it, but after the first day with Devon, I realized I wanted to keep seeing him. I felt like I was doing something important, you know? Something meaningful."

Darcy nodded. "It is important."

"I never cared about stuff like this before." Shame trickled down his spine, steadily, like drops of water from a leaky tap. "I was a selfish bastard when I started fighting pro. Once I started winning, I only cared about myself and doing things that benefited *me*. And yeah, I've grown up a lot since then, but like you said, it's not like I'm Mr. Community Outreach or anything." He shrugged. "But I had fun working with your kids, and I love being there for Devon. His dad's in jail, did you know that?"

"Yeah, I did."

He suddenly felt uncomfortable again. "I know what it's like not to have a dad—it sucks. I mean, my uncle did his best, but he wasn't a very good father figure. He drank like a fish, and he was more interested in chasing tail than playing catch with me, or doing any of that other father-son stuff." Reed swallowed, shifting his gaze downcast. "Boys need that, though. Devon needs it. So I figured...yeah...maybe I could be the one to give it to him."

When he glanced over at Darcy, he was startled by the

approval shining in her eyes.

"What?" he mumbled.

"Nothing," she said softly.

Reed knew damn well that whatever was on her mind, it was the farthest thing from *nothing*, but she didn't give him the chance to question it. Instead, she slid closer and kissed him, her slender arms looping around his shoulders to hold him tight.

His heart melted as she peppered his face with kisses. That sweet mouth skimmed his cheeks, his jaw, his earlobe. Reed's cock strained against his zipper, thickening and pulsing when Darcy climbed into his lap and slipped her hot, wet tongue inside his mouth.

As usual, they went from zero to sex. Clothes gone, bodies naked, his dick inside her before he even knew what was happening. Jeez, normally they at least managed to squeeze in *some* foreplay, but tonight Darcy only spared enough time to cover him with a condom before she sank onto his cock and clutched it with the tight vise of her body.

Reed groaned, his head falling back against the cushion as she began to ride him. "Jesus, baby, give a man some warning before you decide to kill him."

The emotion swimming in her gaze sucked the breath right out of his lungs. "I'm seducing you, Reedford. Shut up and enjoy it."

Enjoy it he did. Impossible not to when the most beautiful woman in the world was grinding on him in a slow, sexy rhythm designed to blow his mind.

But there was something different tonight. Something sweet and tender and…loving. She was peering down at him as if she…loved him.

And Lord, the purity of her expression broke the dam inside him, the one he'd put up to stop himself from thinking too hard about his own feelings.

He wasn't just falling for her anymore—he'd fallen.

He'd fallen so frickin' hard, and now he lay flat on his back as the woman he loved—the woman he *adored*—sent him soaring to a plane of ecstasy where nothing but Darcy and happiness existed.

The orgasm rippled through his body and hummed in his blood, summoning a husky moan from his lips. Darcy's eyes only burned brighter as she watched him come apart beneath her.

"You...are *so* sexy...when you come," she squeezed out. Then those mesmerizing eyes took on a thick sheen of pleasure and she shuddered on top of him, her fingers digging into his abs as she cried out in release.

Afterward, she collapsed on his chest, her soft sigh and even softer hair tickling his pecs. Reed rubbed her back, his throat so tight he could barely draw a breath.

I love you.

The words hovered on the tip of his tongue, desperately trying to escape, but he couldn't seem to voice them. Christ, this was the Apple Shulman fiasco all over again. The terror of exposing himself and getting rejected was so powerful it had seized his vocal cords.

He opened his mouth.

Closed it.

Kept rubbing her back.

Man up already.

Reed stifled a groan and ordered the mocking voice in his head to shut the hell up.

He was totally going to do it. He was going to tell her. He just needed a few seconds to gather up his courage.

Finally, he opened his mouth again. Drew a deep breath and exhaled in an unsteady rush.

Then he murmured her name—and realized that she'd fallen asleep in his arms.

Chapter Fifteen

"You're seriously doing this?" Reed sank into the armchair in front of Gage's desk and eyed the other man warily.

His friend nodded. "Yep."

"You're moving in with Skyler."

"Yep."

"After three months of dating."

"Yep."

Reed shook his head in amazement. If the news had come from anyone else, he'd still be shocked, but coming from Gage? Multiply the shock by a million. Gage had avoided commitment for as long as Reed had known him, and now he was moving in with a woman he'd only recently started dating?

"Isn't it a little sudden?" he asked carefully. "I mean, living together is a huge step, bro."

"I know." Gage looked a tad smug as he perched his hip on the edge of the desk and folded his arms over his broad chest. "But it's happening." He shrugged. "Hell, if it were up to me, we'd be walking down the aisle already, but Skyler laughed in my face when I suggested it. She thinks we should try living together before we jump into marriage."

"*Marriage?*" Reed gaped at his friend. "Dude. Were you abducted by aliens? Who are you and what did those bastard aliens do to Gage Holt?"

The other man just chuckled. "I already told you, this is forever. Skyler's the one."

"But…" Reed found himself sputtering. "How are you so sure of that?"

"She's the one," Gage repeated.

His conviction was downright beautiful.

As Reed unhinged his jaw from the floor, Gage moved away from the desk. "Anyway, I just wanted to share that little bit of good news. Gotta find Jesse now and go over the security assignments for tonight."

With that, Gage slid out the door, leaving Reed to shake his head to himself. Wow. Well. Gage had always been an intense motherfucker, so maybe it made sense that the man extended that same intensity to his relationships.

But to be *that* confident about the future? To know without a shred of doubt that Skyler Thompson was the woman for him?

As Reed rose from the chair, thoughts of Darcy crept into his head. It had been two days since he'd almost told her he'd loved her, and in those two days, he'd nearly blurted it out a hundred more times. Fear and insecurities had stopped him each time, but now, as he stood in Gage's office and replayed his friend's words in his head—*she's the one*—he realized he needed to quit being such a coward.

Because he was Gage. And Darcy was Skyler.

And she was the goddamn *one*.

A smile stretched across his face. Darcy was the only woman for him. He'd known it from the moment he'd met her. So why the hell was he so scared to tell her?

She hadn't uttered the word *fling* in a long, long time. And the other night, when she'd looked at him with honest-to-God love in her eyes...yeah, he didn't think he had a damn thing to be scared about. Darcy might not have said it out loud, but he *knew* she felt the same way he did.

Being the first one to show vulnerability was a terrifying notion for him, but he realized it needed to be done. If he opened himself up and told her how he felt, he was confident she'd find the strength to do the same.

Fueled by that confidence, Reed left the office and headed out to the parking lot. The club didn't open for another hour, which gave him plenty of time to drive over to Darcy's, tell her he loved the shit out of her, and make it back in time for opening hour.

Twenty minutes later, his heart pounded as he climbed the front stoop of her building. Rather than wait to be buzzed in, he punched in the code she'd given him and strode through the door, making a beeline for the elevator. When the doors dinged open on the fourth floor, shaky legs carried him all the way to her apartment.

Okay, he could totally do this. So what if he'd never professed his love to a woman? He was thirty years old. It was about time he introduced three new words into his vocabulary.

He reached her door, frowning when he heard Darcy's voice drifting from the apartment. Figuring she was on the phone, he quietly let himself in, not wanting to interrupt her. He'd taken two steps when another voice wafted out of the living room.

"Yes, it's an impulsive move, but I love him, and this feels right."

Shit. It was Skyler.

Reed suppressed an aggravated groan and hesitated in the front hall. No way in hell was he going to do this in front of an audience. His palms were already clammy enough without the added torture of seeing Skyler smirk at him while he dropped an L-bomb.

"Hey, don't knock it 'til you try it," Skyler teased after Darcy murmured something Reed couldn't make out. "I bet it won't be long at all before you're the one moving in with *your* boyfriend."

He edged back to the door, then froze when Darcy's protest echoed through the apartment.

"Reed's not my boyfriend."

The pain that ripped through his chest was strong enough to shred his heart to pieces.

Reed's not my boyfriend.

His body went colder than a glacier, little pinpricks of agony digging into his skin. No, of course he wasn't her boyfriend. He was nothing but her goddamn fling.

How could he have forgotten that?

There was a long pause, and then Darcy spoke again. "He's just…"

Another pause.

This time Reed didn't wait for her to go on, because he was perfectly capable of finishing that sentence all by himself.

He's just a fuck.

He's just the bad boy I'm killing time with until I find my real *boyfriend.*

The jagged pieces of his heart tore up his chest, leaving him bloody and destroyed as he ducked out of the apartment and gingerly latched the door behind him.

In the corridor, he sagged against the wall and dragged both hands over his scalp. Lord, he was such an idiot. He must have misinterpreted all those tender looks she'd given him, all the unspoken words that he'd assumed meant she felt the same way.

ASS. U. ME.

Yup, what a perfect fucking phrase, but luckily the

universe had stepped in before he'd made an even bigger ass of himself by confessing his love to a woman who thought he was…"just…"—he wasn't even going to bother filling in that heartbreaking blank again.

Setting his jaw, Reed stalked to the elevator and punched the *down* button, then waited for the doors to open and marched right through them.

All without a backward glance.

...

Darcy bit her lip as Skyler's knowing blue eyes twinkled from the other end of the couch.

"He's just what?" the other woman teased.

"He's just…" Darcy gasped. "…my *boyfriend*." Her eyes widened. "Holy shit, he's my boyfriend."

"And?" Skyler prompted.

"And I love him." Her pulse quickened. "Damn it, Skyler, I love him."

"Hey, why are you angry at *me*? Actually, why are you angry *at all*?"

"I'm not angry. I'm…"

She shook her head a couple times, hoping it would knock her jumbled thoughts into balance.

She was in love with Reed. When on earth had *that* happened?

But no, she knew exactly when it happened—when he'd shown her the true meaning of passion. When he'd opened up to her about the loneliness of childhood and how hard it had been to grow up without parents. When he'd taken a little boy under his wing and given him the father figure he'd craved.

When those deep blue eyes locked with hers.

When their lips met.

When…God, whenever she was with him.

Reed Miller might not have looked like her ideal mate on the surface, but Darcy knew without a doubt that he was perfect for her. He challenged her, he thrilled her, he made her feel alive in a way no other man ever had.

"Do you think he loves me back?" she blurted out.

Skyler responded with a soft laugh. "Oh, Darce, you better believe it. Trust me, I saw the way Reed looked at you when you were dating AJ. He had it bad. And he has it even worse now. That man is infatuated with you."

Her teeth worried her lower lip again. "Yeah, but does he *love* me?"

"Why don't you ask him yourself?" Skyler hopped off the sofa with a burst of energy. "I was just about to visit Gage at the club. Why don't you come with me and talk to Reed?"

Darcy's legs felt weak as her friend tugged her onto her feet. Talk to Reed? And say what? That she *loved* him?

What if he didn't say it back?

"I don't know," she said uneasily. "Maybe I should think about it some more before I talk to him."

"Think about what?" Skyler tipped her head. "You told me that he hinted he wanted more, right?"

"Yeah, he *hinted*. I reminded him that it was a fling, and he said *for now*." She swallowed. "That doesn't mean he wants a relationship."

"Darce, that's *totally* what it means." Skyler gave a stern clap of her hands. "Stop being a wuss. You're coming with me to Sin, and you're going to talk to Reed."

It was obvious the other woman wasn't going to take no for an answer. Skyler all but dragged Darcy out the door and pushed her into the elevator, and then she did the same in the parking lot when she shoved Darcy into the passenger seat of the car.

A moment later, Skyler sat behind the wheel, smiling happily as she drove toward the club, while Darcy wrung her hands together with growing anxiety.

This was precisely what she'd been so afraid of. Getting attached. Falling in love. But those fears had been based on her old opinion of Reed, when she'd believed he was shallow, reckless, and temporary. Being with him had shown her a whole different side to the man, and he *had* been hinting that he was interested in more than a casual affair. She'd been the one holding back, but the insufferable man had broken all of her ground rules and bulldozed through her defenses, until her guard was down and her heart was wide open.

Darcy didn't say much during the drive, but it didn't matter, because Skyler chatted about her plans to move into Gage's townhouse and all the preparations she had to make. By the time they arrived at Sin, Darcy's nerves had begun to ebb. The fact that they were in the parking lot didn't hurt, either—it only reminded her of the night Reed had ravished her in the backseat of her car, and the thrilling memory brought a grin to her lips.

Yeah, life with Reed was nothing if not thrilling. She couldn't believe she'd even considered *not* keeping him around.

"Ha, look who's in a good mood now," Skyler teased as they strode through the club's back door. "You're totally thinking about all the lovey dovey sex you guys are going to have tonight, huh?"

She grinned. "Guilty as charged."

Since Reed could usually be found in his office pouring over invoices and timesheets while Gage worked security on the floor, the two women parted ways in the hallway. Skyler ducked into the club through a staff door in the hall, Darcy headed for the stairs at the end of it, but before she could climb the first step, AJ appeared at the top of the staircase.

"Hey," he greeted her, bounding down the stairs to plant a warm and totally platonic kiss on her cheek. "If you're looking for Reed, he's serving tonight."

She furrowed her brow. "How come?"

AJ shrugged. "No clue. He just said he was feeling too antsy to be stuck at his desk and announced that I was gonna have company behind the bar." He touched her arm. "I need to duck outside and help the guys unload a liquor delivery. Go on ahead. Reed'll be happy to see you."

She sure hoped so.

And she also hoped he'd be able to take a break so they could speak in private. The last thing Darcy wanted to do was tell him how she felt by screaming over a deafening dance beat.

The club had only been open for ten minutes, so it wasn't at all crowded when Darcy emerged into the shadowy space. She immediately spotted Reed at the bar, her heart beating faster at the sight of him.

And then not beating at all when she saw what he was doing.

His roped arms rested on the sleek counter as he leaned in to whisper something in the ear of a very pretty, very busty brunette in a skimpy halter top. Miss Thang was sitting on a stool with her legs crossed and her indecently short miniskirt riding up her thighs, a throaty giggle piercing the air as she responded to whatever Reed had said.

Darcy's body went cold. Was he seriously flirting with another woman? Right in front of her?

Granted, he hadn't seen her yet. But *still*.

Gritting her teeth in anger, she marched up to the bar, halting two feet from the brunette.

Reed's expression didn't change when he noticed her. His rogue grin stayed in place, and he tipped his head in greeting. "Hey, Darce." Then, to her staggering shock, he turned right back to the brunette and said, "Anyway, I want to know more about this modeling agency of yours."

Darcy's mouth fell open. "Are you *kidding* me?"

The rage simmering in her stomach only burned hotter when she glimpsed the irritation in his eyes. "Hold that thought, baby girl," he drawled to the other woman. "I've gotta take care of something."

Baby girl?

Darcy had never been more insulted in her life as Reed drifted to the far edge of the bar, gesturing for her to follow. Her hands trembled and her throat closed up, hurt and anger forming a lethal cocktail inside her.

"What the hell is going on?" she demanded once they were out of the brunette's earshot.

He had the nerve to look confused. "I'm just talking to a customer."

"Talking?" she echoed in disbelief. "You're hitting on that woman!"

Reed paused. Then he twisted the knife harder. "Yeah. I guess I am."

A volatile wave of emotion slammed into her chest. She was horrified and humiliated to feel tears stinging her eyes, and she blinked wildly to keep them at bay. "What's going on, Reed?" she whispered. "What is this?"

It was early enough in the night that the music was at a normal level, and she knew he heard her anguished plea.

He responded with a light shrug. "I think this is the fling running its course, babe."

Her heart plummeted to the pit of her stomach like a sack of bricks. "Are you serious?"

Another pause. Then he nodded.

Darcy was speechless. She stared at him, trying desperately to understand what was happening. She'd come here to tell this man she *loved* him, and now he was telling her it was *over*?

"It was bound to happen, Darce. I mean, you said so

yourself, this was never going to lead to a relationship."

His tone was so nonchalant she almost picked up an empty glass from the counter and hurled it at his smug, unfeeling face.

"I think it's time we both moved on to greener and better pastures," Reed said with another infuriating shrug.

And then, right in front of her wide eyes, he had the nerve to tilt his head in the brunette's direction and shoot Darcy a wink.

As if they were two bros talking about scoring a hot lay for the evening.

"Are you *kidding* me?"

This time the incredulous shout came not from Darcy, but from Skyler, who appeared behind them just in time to catch Reed's last remark and thoughtless grin.

Reed looked annoyed again. "What now?"

The younger woman charged forward and wrapped a protective arm around Darcy's shoulders. "You're a real bastard, Reed, you know that?" Skyler sounded livid as she glowered at him.

"Hell. This is why flings are such stupidly terrible ideas." Reed sighed as he addressed Darcy. "Look, we had our fun, okay? Now it's time to call it a day and have fun with other people."

With that, he strode off in the direction of the brunette.

He didn't look back. Not even once.

Darcy made a valiant effort not to cry, biting her lip so hard the metallic taste of blood filled her mouth.

"Oh my God," Skyler murmured. "I can't believe…" She gave Darcy's shoulder a comforting squeeze. "I'm so sorry, Darce. I want you to forget every single word I said back at your place. He's not worth it. I promise you, he's not worth it."

Her entire body had gone numb. Her gaze stayed fixed on Reed, who was once again leaning over the counter, a devilish grin playing on his lips as he flirted with another woman. When he reached out and tucked a strand of hair behind the brunette's ear, Darcy's heart officially shattered into a million pieces.

"Will you drive me home?" she blurted out.

Sympathy swam in Skyler's eyes. "Oh, Darce."

"Please, Sky." She gritted her teeth so hard her molars ached. "Just take me home."

With a nod, Skyler tightened her grip around her shoulders and quietly led her away from the bar.

Chapter Sixteen

A dark cloud loomed over him. No, wait. Make that *two* dark clouds.

Reed squinted from his perch on the couch, his head spinning like a carousel as he tried to bring his eyes into focus. The two figures above him slowly merged into one, as his double vision snapped back to normal. Christ. It felt like someone was pounding his temples with a chisel. How much had he had to drink last night?

A lot.

No kidding, he almost snapped at the sardonic inner voice. But even the act of *thinking* it made his head hurt, and a wave of nausea swept over him in response.

"Get up."

The icy command was uttered by a familiar voice, and though it hadn't been loud, to his aching head it sounded like a banshee's shriek.

"Lower your voice," he groaned, reaching up to rub his throbbing temples.

AJ didn't sound at all sympathetic. "Jesus Christ, man.

Did you drink all that? In one sitting?"

Reed's gaze shifted to the coffee table, which boasted two empty pints of whiskey and a half-finished fifth of scotch. It was all the alcohol he'd had in the house, and the liquor cabinet had been the first thing he'd opened when he'd come home last night. His goal had been to drink Darcy Grant right out of his heart, and it looked like he'd succeeded. With the drinking part, at least. But exorcising Darcy from his heart?

He'd failed miserably.

The shame of what he'd done to her, combined with the agony of knowing he'd lost her, fused together and somehow turned into a sharp dose of anger, directed at the man hovering over him.

"You told me to prove it to her," Reed accused.

AJ blinked in confusion. "What are you talking about?"

"Darcy. You told me to prove to her that I'd changed, to show her that I was someone she could fall for. Why the *fuck* did you say that?" Groaning, Reed heaved himself off the couch and onto his feet. His entire body immediately swayed, the floor beneath him and the walls around him spinning wildly. "Shit. I'm gonna hurl."

Before he threw up all over himself—or AJ—he managed to lurch into the hall bathroom. On his knees, he emptied three bottles' worth of alcohol into the toilet, then draped himself over the bowl, dry heaving until the vicious contractions of his stomach finally ceased.

He heard footsteps, cursing when AJ appeared in the open doorway. His friend wore a look of sheer disgust, mingled with a flicker of bewilderment.

"I have no idea what you're babbling about," AJ announced. "All I know is that you left us in the lurch on Friday night, and you didn't bother showing up for work today, either."

"Today? What time is it?" Reed said weakly.

AJ scowled. "It's eight."

"AM or PM?"

"PM, goddamn it!"

Shit. He'd been passed out on the couch for…his brain valiantly tried to do the math. He'd started drinking around ten on Friday…crashed around two…so that meant… eighteen hours. He'd been in an alcohol-induced coma for eighteen frickin' hours.

The guilt rose fast, making him gag again, but there was nothing left to throw up.

"And don't get me started on what you did to Darcy," AJ was fuming from the door.

Like he could ever forget. Reed's cheek still stung from where Skyler had slapped it. Gage's girlfriend had driven right back to Sin after she'd left with Darcy, and like a mama lioness, she'd ripped into Reed good, so furious with him that Gage had been forced to step in and pry her off his friend.

That was when Reed had hightailed it out of the club, but he didn't remember much after that.

"I did the only thing I could do to save my dignity," he mumbled to AJ. "And you…screw you, man."

"Screw *me*?" AJ echoed in disbelief.

Reed managed to stagger to his feet. "Yeah, screw *you*. I did what you said—I *showed* her. I showed her everything, every goddamn part of me, and you know what? She *still* didn't want me." He stumbled to the sink, where he rinsed out his mouth and splashed cold water on his face, then spoke again without looking at his friend. "Give me a minute to shower, and then I'll head over to the club."

"No way." The response was swift and firm. "You're not going anywhere until you tell me what happened. No more of this confusing babbling. Straight up, Reed—why the hell did you cheat on her?"

His jaw fell open, but he supposed he shouldn't have been

surprised by the accusation. He'd all but dangled that woman under Darcy's nose, making it clear what he intended to do. But the fact that AJ thought he'd actually gone through with it only illustrated what Reed had been trying hard not to admit.

His best friends still thought he was a screw-up.

Darcy did, too.

And no amount of "proving" could change any of their minds.

"I guess I cheated on her because that's what I do," he said coldly. "Right, AJ? I cheat on women, and I hire drug dealers to work at our club, and I don't stock the fuckin' bar, but of course, right? It's classic Reed Miller, isn't it, AJ?"

The other man looked momentarily stunned. Then he cleared his throat. "Okay. Enough. Clearly, we need to start over."

"Clearly, we need to get to work," Reed snapped back.

He tried to brush past AJ, but his friend clamped a hand on his shoulder and glared at him. "You're not going anywhere."

Anger climbed up his throat. "AJ—"

"I mean it. You're not taking another step until you tell me exactly what happened last night. From start to fuckin' finish."

...

Ice cream. Lots and lots of ice cream.

Darcy knew from experience that ice cream was the one and only cure for a broken heart. It was sweet enough that it made the bitter taste coating your throat easier to swallow, and if you bought the low-fat kind, you only had to worry about going up *one* dress size instead of the ten you'd gain once you reached your fifth carton.

Oh, and you could eat it for breakfast.

Which was just what Darcy did when she stumbled into her kitchen on Sunday morning. She bypassed the fridge, opened the freezer, and a minute later, she sat at the counter, devouring a pint of triple chocolate mousse right out of the carton.

She hadn't heard from Reed since Friday night.

She didn't expect to hear from him.

Nope, he'd made it more than clear that he was finished with her. Like she was a piece of trash to him, easily discarded and unworthy of any further consideration.

Well, at least she'd learned her lesson—always, always, *always* listen to your mother.

Her mom had told her this would happen. She'd warned her not to date a man Darcy didn't see a future with unless she was absolutely sure of that outcome. Though, in Darcy's defense, she *hadn't* seen a future with Reed, not at the start, anyway. It wasn't until much, much later that she'd begun to question herself.

God, she was such an idiot. For one foolish moment, she'd actually believed there might be more to Reed Miller than met the eye, that he *wasn't* a self-absorbed, sex-crazed playboy with a no-strings mentality and a thirst for the chase.

But yep, he was. He totally was. And being right had never felt so awful.

Darcy shoveled another spoonful of ice cream into her mouth and groaned with pleasure. "Oh, Ben and Jerry," she mumbled to the carton. "What would I do without you? Why can't one of you be my boyfriend?"

The carton did not respond.

But for a split second, she actually thought she heard it say her name.

It took a few head-scratching seconds to realize that someone *was* calling her name, only the voice was coming from the front door.

Frowning, she slid off the breakfast stool and headed for the hall, where she heard a loud rap on the door, then another irritated, "Darcy!"

She swallowed a groan when she recognized AJ's voice. Wonderful. Had her ex-boyfriend decided to stop by to rub her breakup with Reed in her face?

No, she realized. No way would AJ ever do that. It wasn't his style.

Besides, he sounded more angry than gloaty at the moment.

Darcy opened the door and glared at him. "What do you want?"

"Wow. That's wicked rude," he marveled. "I'm going to let it slide, though, because I'm about to be ruder."

AJ pushed his way inside, his six-foot frame hovering over her as he folded his arms across his chest. "What the *hell* is the matter with you?"

Her jaw dropped. "Excuse me?"

"You heard me." He shook his head in disapproval. "I'm really disappointed in you. Reed is a good guy, and to just throw him away like that? Dick move, Darce. *Dick. Move.*"

Shock crashed into her. "Are you serious? *I* threw *him* away? I hate to burst your self-righteous bubble, AJ, but it was the other way around!"

She spun on her heel and marched back to the kitchen, making a beeline for her Ben and Jerry's. The nerve of him! To imply that *she'd* done something wrong? When it was *Reed* who'd been picking up another chick right in front of her Friday night?

Darcy stuck the spoon in the carton, scooped up some chocolatey goodness, and shoved it in her mouth. When she heard AJ's footsteps in the doorway, she lifted her head so she could glare at him again.

"Your 'good guy' best friend dumped me Friday night,"

she said through a mouthful of ice cream. "Get your facts straight."

"He only did that because you decided he wasn't good enough to be your boyfriend," AJ retorted, accusation hanging from his voice.

She gaped at him. "That's crazy."

"He *heard* you, Darce."

"I have no idea what you're talking about." Setting down her spoon, she matched AJ's pose and crossed her arms.

Sighing, her ex-boyfriend approached the counter and propped his hip up against it. "It was total chaos after you left on Friday. Reed was moping around like the sky had fallen, but refused to tell anyone why, and then Skyler showed back up and flipped out on him, accusing him of some seriously nasty shit. Then *Gage* got caught in the middle, and eventually Reed just up and left the club—on our busiest frickin' night!"

Darcy couldn't conjure up even a smidgen of sympathy. "Gee, I'm *so* sorry."

AJ scowled at her. "Anyway, he didn't show up for work yesterday either, which is totally unlike him, so I went over to his place and found him shit-faced on his couch."

The sarcasm continued to ooze out. "Oh no. Poor Reed."

"Christ. It's like dealing with children," AJ mumbled, before his expression snapped back to somber. "Look, it took a while, but I finally managed to get the truth out of him."

She faltered, the hard front she'd been putting on slipping slightly. "The truth?"

"He told me he came by your place on Friday right before the club opened. He overheard you talking to Skyler about how he's not boyfriend material or some shit, and how you don't want a relationship with him."

Darcy's breath hitched. "Wait, that can't be right."

"That's what he says happened. And after he heard that, he decided he might as well end it with you before you ended it with *him*." AJ sighed again. "It's a guy thing. Self-preservation and all that stuff."

She couldn't believe what she was hearing. Reed had come by on Friday? How was that possible? He hadn't knocked, and she certainly hadn't heard him come in. And if he really *had* stopped by, then why hadn't he heard the *rest* of her conversation with Skyler? The part where she'd waxed poetic about how much she loved him and confessed her fear that he might not love her back.

"But…but I told Skyler I was in love with him," she stammered, feeling a tad awkward to be revealing it to AJ. "How come he didn't hear *that*?"

"I guess he left before you got to that part," AJ said flatly.

"So he decided to get back at me by hitting on another woman?" she grumbled.

"He wasn't getting back at you. He was just kick-starting the inevitable."

The inevitable… Reed had thought she was going to break up with him. Despite her irritation over his heartless method of protecting himself, Darcy's heart ached at the notion that she'd made Reed believe she didn't care about him.

"I'm so stupid," she blurted out, swallowing a lump of frustration. "Why did I keep calling it a fling when I knew it had turned into something more?"

AJ chuckled. "You were in denial?" he suggested.

"I was. I totally was." She moaned in misery. "Crap, I need to go and talk to him. Do you know if he's home?"

"No, he mentioned something about hanging out with some kid named Devon today. Or maybe it was Kevin?" AJ offered a blank look. "Can't remember the name. I had no idea he was doing that Big Brother program, but it's pretty cool, huh? Oh, I think they're meeting at the park behind your school."

Darcy was already dashing to the doorway. "Can you let

yourself out?" she called over her shoulder. "I've gotta throw some clothes on."

AJ's soft laughter tickled her back, but she ignored it. Her mind was already a million miles away, every fiber of her being focused on Reed and what she would say to him when she saw him.

Yes, he'd acted like a total jerk the other night, and she certainly wasn't letting him off the hook for it, but now that she understood where he'd been coming from, she couldn't bring herself to stay mad at him. She loved him, damn it. And she was pretty certain he felt the same way about her.

Now she just had to find out if she was right.

Darcy halted in the middle of her bedroom, a smile breaking out on her face as she experienced a stroke of brilliance.

She knew *just* what she had to do.

Chapter Seventeen

"That was the worst pass on the planet!" Devon's laughing taunt floated across the field and penetrated Reed's distracted thoughts.

Shit, he must have spaced out. He couldn't even remember *throwing* the football, let alone what the pass had looked like.

"Why don't we take a breather?" Reed called out.

He felt like an ass for putting a stop to the game, but at the moment, he was way too preoccupied to focus on football. Or Devon. Or anything that didn't start with D and end with A-R-C-Y.

He was such a mess. He'd been wallowing in self-pity ever since Darcy had stumbled out of the club the other night. The devastated look on her face had been branded into his memory. At the time, though, it had seemed like the only solution. The only way to permanently sever the hold Darcy Grant had on his heart.

If she hated him, then she wouldn't fight his decision to break things off.

If she hated him, then maybe he'd finally be able to get

over her.

She didn't want a relationship, and he didn't want a fling. If he'd kept seeing her, they'd be forever in a standoff. His feelings for her would only have gotten stronger, which meant his heart would only break harder when she decided to move on. So he'd decided to end it first.

And boy, had he ended it. Reed still felt like throwing up when he remembered how he'd forced himself to flirt with that faceless girl, all the while feeling Darcy's betrayed blue eyes boring a hole into him. It had been torture, but he'd made himself do it. Made himself live up to the selfish asshole label Darcy had pinned on him the day they'd met.

"Hey! Ms. Grant! Reed, look, Ms. Grant is here!"

Devon's voice once again pierced through the fog, jolting Reed back to reality.

Wait—Darcy is here?

His frantic gaze swept over the football field, his heart jumping to his throat when he spotted her. She stood near the home team's bench, wearing skinny jeans, a black tank top, and bright red flats on her feet. The splash of color brought a smile to his lips. Lord, he loved that about her. The way her adventurous nature seeped out of that good girl exterior, the hint of naughtiness beneath her well-behaved surface.

He was rooted in place as their gazes locked, but neither one of them made a move to approach the other.

Devon, on the other hand, had no problem running over to Darcy. The boy flung his arms around her waist and hugged her, and Reed's heart squeezed as he watched her return the playful embrace.

Their murmured voices carried over to him, but he couldn't make out their words. A groove dug into his forehead when he saw Darcy kneel down and whisper something in Devon's ear. There was a flash of movement, as if she'd slipped something into the boy's hand, but they were too far away for

Reed to see what had exchanged hands.

A second later, Devon sprinted toward him.

Darcy stayed put, and Reed's bewilderment grew. He flashed her a questioning look, but all he got in return was a tiny shrug and what looked like a very mischievous smile.

His pulse sped up, even though he knew better than to think…to think what? Darcy's presence made no sense to him. She was supposed to hate him, damn it. So why was she standing twenty feet away *smiling* at him?

Devon skidded to a stop at Reed's feet, clutching a little green golf pencil and a folded piece of white paper in his small hand. "Here," the boy announced, thrusting out his arm. "This is for you."

Reed held his breath as he accepted the paper. He was also embarrassed to discover that his fingers were trembling wildly as he slowly unfolded the note.

When he saw what was written on it, his nerves vanished and his breath came shuddering out on a laugh.

In her feminine handwriting, Darcy had written three words that made his heart soar.

I love you.

Below that, she'd drawn two boxes, one for yes, one for no.

She'd checked *yes*.

And circled it half a dozen times.

"What does it say?" Devon demanded, standing on his tiptoes and craning his head to try and take a peek.

Reed laughed as he scanned the rest of the note, which posed a question.

Do you love me?

Two boxes. Yes or no.

As his pulse drummed between his ears, he refolded the note and tucked it along with the pencil in his pocket, then glanced at Devon. "Wait here a second, my man. I've gotta go kiss your teacher."

"Ewwwwww!"

The boy's horrified wail followed Reed all the way to Darcy, who patiently waited for him to approach.

When he reached her, she cocked her head, a move that caused her hair to cascade over her shoulder. "I spoke to AJ."

He sighed. "Why am I not surprised?"

"Don't be mad at him. He was just being a good friend. To both of us."

Reed thought about how AJ had dragged him off the couch yesterday and sobered him up, and his heart squeezed at the memory. "He's a damn good friend," he said hoarsely.

There was a beat of silence.

"I didn't see you check off a box," she murmured, her blue eyes searching his face.

"That's because I didn't have to."

Her brows knitted in confusion.

Reed smiled. "I don't need to tell you how I feel on a piece of paper, baby. I'm not too scared to say the words out loud."

Her breath caught.

Reed stepped closer and swept his fingers along the delicate edge of her jaw, his voice coming out hoarse. "I love you."

Darcy's entire face lit up. "You do?"

"So fucking much," he said solemnly.

The smile she rewarded him with was so damn radiant he wished he'd brought his sunglasses. "Thank God," she blurted out.

Chuckling, Reed touched her cheek. "What, you were afraid I wouldn't say it back?"

"Terrified," she confessed. "Especially after…"

Regret clamped around his throat. "I'm so sorry for the other night, Darce. I was a total jerk. But I need you to know that nothing happened with that girl. I walked away from her the second you were gone." He swallowed. "I just needed you to believe that I was over you. It was the only way for me to…"

A soft smile tugged on her lips as he voiced the familiar phrase, but this time she wasted no time finishing it for him. "For you to protect your heart. I get it, Reed. AJ told me you heard me and Skyler talking." She shook her head. "And I think we need to have a little talk about eavesdropping."

"I know," he groaned, lowering his gaze to avoid her reprimanding look. "I shouldn't have—"

"If you're going to eavesdrop," she interrupted primly, "as least eavesdrop on the *whole* conversation."

His head jerked up. "What?"

"If you'd stayed for five seconds more, you would have heard me telling Skyler that yes, you *were* my boyfriend, and that I was madly, passionately, ridiculously in love with you."

His heartbeat accelerated. "Really?"

"Really."

"Aw, hell. I can't even eavesdrop properly. I really am a dumbass, huh?"

Her melodic laughter wrapped around him like a warm blanket. "Yep, you are. But I forgive you." She paused. "Do you forgive me for being such a jerk about the whole fling thing and laying down all those rules?"

"There's nothing to forgive," he said simply. "You wanted passion, I gave you passion. But you also happened to get something else out of the deal." He traced the seam of her lips with his finger. "You got love, babe. Lots and lots of love."

"Aww, I think that's the sweetest thing you've ever said to me, Reedford."

His lips twitched. "One of these days you're going to have to accept that *Reedford* isn't my full name."

"Oh, shut it. You love it when I call you that."

God help him, but he couldn't deny it. "Fine," he said, pretending to cave. "I guess I can live with it."

She beamed at him. "Good. Now will you kiss me already?"

Ha. Like he could ever say no to this woman.

Reed's mouth came down on hers, their lips meeting in a kiss that went from sweet and gentle to hot and passionate in a single heartbeat. But just as his tongue filled her mouth, an outraged cry broke through the haze of lust.

"Ewwwwww! I am *so* telling my mom about this!"

Reed wrenched his mouth away from Darcy and turned to scowl at the kid who'd appeared at their side. "Don't you dare," he warned the boy. "Otherwise, I'll tell her all about the way you blackmailed me into buying you a second ice cream cone last weekend."

Devon blinked. "Got it. I saw nothing. Nothing at all."

"Pleasure doing business with you, kid."

Darcy choked out a laugh. "So…what do you boys have planned for the rest of the day?"

"We were going to get pizza next," Devon informed her. "Wanna come?"

She hesitated. "I don't want to intrude. I mean, this is guy time…"

Devon grinned widely. "Naah, you won't intrude. You can be one of the guys. C'mon, let's go."

As the boy bounded toward the parking lot, Reed took Darcy's hand and tugged her close. "You can be one of the guys…for now," he amended. "But afterward? You turn back into a woman. *My* woman."

She shivered when his lips brushed her earlobe, and he couldn't help taking a teasing bite. "Hmmm. Out of curiosity, what does being your woman entail exactly?"

He flashed a wicked smile. "It means that when I get you home, you'll be underneath me. Or on top of me. Or any other position that allows my cock to sink into that sexy body of yours." His tone echoed with challenge. "Got a problem with that?"

Darcy answered in a breathless tone. "Not. At. All."

Epilogue

She was at the bar, sandwiched between a twenty-something guy in a red trucker hat and a pair of giggling, tipsy women. The martini she'd ordered was half-empty. She'd been sitting on this stool for more than ten minutes, wearing a dress so short her ass was nearly hanging out of it, yet nobody had come over to hit on her, which didn't do much for her ego.

Darcy pursed her lips, then took another sip, her gaze wandering around the shadowy main floor of the Krib. A hip-hop track with the filthiest lyrics she'd ever heard served as the backdrop for a sea of grinding dancers and couples tucked away pawing at each other.

And she was all alone like a chump.

"'Scuse me."

Or not.

A muscular male form wedged in between her and Trucker Hat, resting one defined forearm on the counter. A hint of spicy cologne wafted toward her as the man leaned in close.

"Hi."

Darcy appraised him for a moment before responding. "Hi."

Blue eyes smoldered at her. "Can I buy you a drink?"

She gestured to her glass. "Already have one."

"Hmmm." He slanted his head, pausing in thought.

From the corner of her eye, Darcy noticed the two women at her side watching the interaction with visible curiosity.

"All right…how about I fuck you instead?"

Loud, dual gasps sounded from Darcy's right. A deeply impressed look came from Trucker Hat on the left.

"I don't even know your name," she said slowly.

"I'm Reed." He extended a hand, one eyebrow cocked.

After a moment, she shook his hand, shivering when his thumb stroked the inside of her palm. "I'm Darcy."

Reed's mouth quirked in a rogue smile. "Do you want me to fuck you, Darcy?"

The women beside her were damn near holding their breaths. Darcy decided to make them squirm for a few seconds, just for the heck of it.

Then she met Reed's magnetic eyes and said, "Yes. I would."

Hand still gripping hers, he helped her off the stool. The customers at the counter watched them with wide eyes, and Darcy had to fight a wave of laughter. She and Reed had played a lot of naughty games in the six months they'd been together, but this was one of her favorites. Making jaws drop was a lot more fun than she'd thought it would be.

As they drifted away from the bar, Trucker Hat's amazed voice tickled Darcy's back. "Holy crap—I can't believe that worked!"

"Some chicks are just that easy," one of the women said haughtily.

The laugh she'd been holding flew out. "Did you hear that? Apparently I'm easy," Darcy murmured into Reed's ear.

He grinned. "Just the way I like you, baby."

The music pounded, vibrating in her blood as she and Reed headed for the exit. He'd slung his arm around her, his large hand splaying at the small of her back, firm and possessive. When they stepped outside into the frigid February air, Darcy instantly shivered. She hadn't brought a coat, and her dress was so flimsy she may as well have been naked. Fortunately, Reed's Camaro was parked at the curb, and it was warm and toasty when she slid into the passenger seat.

"So," her bad boy said as he settled behind the wheel. "Choose your poison."

Licking her lips, she reached across the center console and palmed the bulge in his pants. "I choose this one."

He snorted. "That's a given, babe. But you know how it is—location, location, location. So what'll it be? Hotel? Your place? Mine? The car?"

She flashed a coy smile. "You pick. I'm easy, remember?"

An almost reverent expression filled his handsome face. It was how he always looked at her, especially when he was about to say a particular sequence of words.

"God, I love you."

Yep, those were the words. They never failed to make her heart soar, and she would never, ever get tired of hearing them.

"Love you too, Reedford." She smacked a loud kiss on his cheek before giving his groin a hearty squeeze. "I have an idea. Why don't we start with the hotel, and then see if we can check the rest of the locations off the list before the night is over?"

His grin went downright wicked. "Challenge accepted."

Then he started the engine and spent the whole night proving to her that there was no challenge Reed Miller couldn't meet.

About the Author

A RITA-award-nominated, best-selling author, Elle Kennedy grew up in the suburbs of Toronto, Ontario, and holds a BA in English from York University. From an early age, she knew she wanted to be a writer and actively began pursuing that dream when she was a teenager. She loves strong heroines and sexy alpha heroes, and just enough heat and danger to keep things interesting!

Elle loves to hear from her readers. Visit her website www.ellekennedy.com or sign up for her newsletter to receive updates about upcoming books and exclusive excerpts. You can also find her on Facebook or follow her on Twitter (@ElleKennedy).

Discover Elle Kennedy's **After Hours** *series...*

ONE NIGHT OF SIN

ONE NIGHT OF TROUBLE

If you love sexy romance, one-click these steamy Brazen releases...

RULES OF A REBOUND
a *Breakup Bash* novel by Nina Crespo

Natalie Winters is celebrating her divorce with her friends at the Breakup Bash when she meets security specialist turned bartender Rome Collier. He's strong, protective…and hot—everything she's ever wanted in a man. But can she convince him—and herself—hat he's more than just a rebound?

WRONG BED, RIGHT GIRL
an *Accidental Love* novel by Rebecca Brooks

Falling head-first into the wrong woman's bed was not how Reed Bishop's night was supposed to go. Now a gorgeous, half-naked ballet dancer was threatening his manhood…with a book. He can't blame her. He'd just been doing his job, tracking down his lead informant, but the mixup staying in her apartment was no longer safe. Now the totally off-limits Talia is sleeping in his bed while he tosses and turns on the couch.

Dirty Deal
a *Perfectly Matched* novel by Christine Bell

Matchmaker Serena Elliott helps clients find love, but when it comes to her own love life, she believes in getting in and getting out before things turn complicated. Bidding on army doctor Bryan Metcalf at a charity auction is just a means to an end, but Bryan has other ideas. If he's to spend his leave in peace, he needs Serena to play his fake girlfriend. But there are other forces at work that believe these two belong together, and they just might find out that happily ever afters *do* exist.

Two Week Seduction
a novel by Kathy Lyons

Former bad boy turned Tech Sergeant John O'Donnell has exactly two weeks to sort out his mother's finances before he heads back overseas—two weeks that he's determined to spend as far from his best friend's little sister as possible. Alea Heling has been craving more from John since their wild days together in high school, and this time, she's not taking no for an answer… even if John won't let it become more. Even if more is what they both need.